The Super-secret Diary of HOLLY HOPKINSON

A little bit of a BIG disaster!

BOOKS BY CHARLIE P. BROOKS

THE SUPER-SECRET DIARY OF HOLLY HOPKINSON:

THIS IS GOING TO BE A FIASCO!

A LITTLE BIT OF A BIG DISASTER!

The Super-secret Diary of HOLLY HOPKINSON

A little bit of a BIG disaster!

CHARLIE P. BROOKS
and KATY RIDDELL

HarperCollins *Children's Books*

First published in Great Britain by
HarperCollins *Children's Books* in 2021
HarperCollins *Children's Books* is a division of HarperCollins*Publishers* Ltd
1 London Bridge Street
London SE1 9GF

www.harpercollins.co.uk

HarperCollins*Publishers*
1st Floor, Watermarque Building, Ringsend Road
Dublin 4, Ireland

1

HB ISBN 978-0-00-832812-2
PB ISBN 978-0-00-832815-3

A CIP catalogue record for this title is available from the British Library.
Typeset in Stempel Schneidler Std 12.5pt/18pt by Sorrel Packham

Printed and bound in the UK using 100% renewable electricity
at CPI Group (UK) Ltd

MIX
Paper from
responsible sources

FSC
www.fsc.org

FSC™ C007454

To Caroline

CHARACTERS

HOLLY
HOPKINSON

VINNIE

DAD

AUNT
ELECTRA

PROLOGUE

THIS IS VOLUME II OF HOLLY HOPKINSON'S
OFFICIAL MEMOIRS, RECORDING THE
LIFE AND TIMES OF THE HOPKINSON
FAMILY - ONCE OF LONDON TOWN.

I have hidden Volume I in a
time capsule (biscuit tin) in
Grandpa's farmyard, away
from prying eyes. It will be
a minefield of information
for scholars in future years.

No one could have predicted four months ago
that the Hopkinson family would be banished to
a whiffy farmhouse with a haunted attic in the
middle of a field somewhere near a town called
Chipping Topley; all because my doofus dad lost
his job.

We have survived so far. But there is a ghost in the locked attic called Mabel, who Grandpa says is very cross, so we're not allowed to go up there.

And cleanliness is a long-forgotten cherished friend, so the chances of us being flipping well wiped out by a virus are high.

There will be TV camera crews and people in white suits wearing masks trampling around our farmyard while helicopters hover overhead making a double-whopper racket.

Mum is still computing* back to London and having the odd sleepover. Dad says she stays up all night talking about books that she hasn't read.

Not only is Mum a big cheese in the PR world, she 'doesn't let the grass get mown round her feet' when she's at home either.

Mum is getting quite BIG on the Village Cultural Events Organising Committee (VCEOC). Dad says she likes controlling everything and that she's got Oh Cee Dee, but she doesn't have a cough or anything.

* COMPUTING –
working on the train.

2

Talking of Dad, he went through a bad stage when we came to the farm – way too much screen time and stuff like that. But he's bought the Chequers in Lower Goring, our local pub, and he's going to turn it into a bistro pub with the skills he learned from the daytime TV cooking programmes.

So he's happy now, which is GOOD, because, as a kid, Holly Hopkinson (schoolchild) can only be as happy as my unhappiest parent.

Grandpa is on a roll after he sold his foal, High Five, to the queen for a 'prince's sum'.

Grandpa has decided to buy more horses, which are apparently much more risky than cows but less likely to trample all over you in the field. Anyway, Grandpa will be needing the services of Holly Hopkinson Racing Manager Inc.

HOLLY HOPKINSON
BAND MANAGER
INC.

My brother Harold is now lead singer and drummer in his band, so he has to shout to make himself heard.

Holly Hopkinson Band Manager Inc. is officially their manager according to my contracts. I now have a smart mobile phone, but I double-whopper desperately need an iPad to run my business empire with – RAPIDO, as they say in Chile.

Harold and his mate Stickly can't agree on a name for the band, so I think there's a real possibility they might split up. And Stickly wants to recruit another member to take 'some of the load'. Anyone would think they were a bunch of removal men.

My sister Harmony is swooning around Stickly like a moose when she's meant to be writing songs. And she's still into protesting big time – even though we can't get much internet service on the farm.

4

Aunt Electra is officially thinking of leaving Bohemia and coming to be general manager of the Chequers – that should be a hoot.

We also still have assorted animals, which all do pretty well what they want to WHEN they want to.

BARKLEY

There is:

☆ Barkley, our mutt, who has not settled in well and is pining for the poodle in the park that he used to say rude things to.

☆ Beanstalk, Grandpa's miniature Shetland pony.

BEANSTALK

FLORENCE

☆ Florence, who you can squeeze milk and cheese out of.

 ⭐ A bunch of unruly chickens who lay their Prince Williams* where they flipping well feel like it.

 * **PRINCE WILLIAMS** – boiled eggs. Grandpa likes his with the yolk nice and runny.

 ⭐ Various pigs, sheep and cows that manufacture poo and not much else.

⭐ Moggy, who Mum says is excessively impertinent.

⭐ Which just leaves me, Holly Hopkinson, bringing up the rear of the Hopkinsons as usual. It ISN'T easy being the youngest member of a family, thank you very much. Always fixing everyone's problems and dealing with my best friends.

There's Aleeshaa, my ex-best friend in London, who has been downgraded through her own fault; my current countryside best friend, Daffodil; and Vinnie, my animal friend, who may be due for promotion.

OFFICIAL TOP SECRET –

for those of you who have been living on Planet Zob, a squillion miles away, here is some CLASSIFIED information.

On my tenth birthday the other day my Aunt Electra gave me the **MAGIC POCKET WATCH** with which to navigate the slows and rapids of life. When I wiggle it in front of anyone's nose the RIGHT number of times and say:

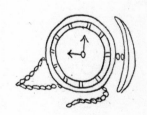

'SPIRO, SPERO, SQUIGGLEOUS SCOTCH,
CAST YOUR EYES WHITHER MY WATCH.'

I can **HYPNOTISE** adults and animals and make them do anything.

BUT THE THING IS,

IT DOESN'T ALWAYS WORK.

CHAPTER 1

SCHOOL REPORTS

TODAY WAS OUR SECOND-TO-LAST DAY AT
LOWER GORING VILLAGE SCHOOL BEFORE
THE CHRISTMAS HOLIDAYS. BUT I HAVE
A LOT ON MY PLATE.

So, now I'm in business, I write LOADS of 'priority lists'.

1. Get some live gigs for Harold's band – he's too dopey to find them himself.

2. Keep an eye on Grandpa, who is buying some horses – as I am his **OFFICIAL** racing and business partner.

3. Get my hands on an iPad.

Miss Bossom – that's our bonkers teacher – was writing our school reports while we did some pointless arts and crafts nonsense.

I happened to notice that she always looks at the kid she's writing about. Bossy Bossom would not make a good spy.

I'll bet that she would squeal as soon as they got the torturing stuff out. One sight of a pair of electrodes and she'd tell anyone where the plans for the secret tunnel were.

She's also DOUBLE-WHOPPER dopey enough to leave the reports that she's written in her top drawer. So when the teachers sloped off for the coffee and biscuits that make their breath smell, I had a 'sneak preview'.

My OFFICIAL countryside best friend Daffodil Chichester's general report was on the top of the pile.

> *Daffodil is a very talented girl, who has an excellent grasp of all her subjects. She also has lovely manners and is very kind. And the class particularly enjoyed Daffodil's last show-and-tell. The scented cushions were so delightful. Daffodil is a pleasure to teach.*

Flipping heck, Bossy is laying it on a bit thick. If you ask me, she's looking for a few free embroidered candles from Mrs Chichester's shop.

The next report was for Vinnie. I assumed that he would be getting a stinker, but I was in for a surprise:

> *Vinnie has made great strides this term and he brings unique talents to the class.*

it said. What a load of tosh. The only things Vinnie brings to the class are snails in his pockets.

If I didn't know better, I'd say that Miss Bossom is after something from Vinnie's grandma Vera, the phantom cake baker, or his Uncle Vince, who is big on the VCEOC.

Then I saw Felicity Snoop's report.

> *Felicity has been such a help again this term. What would we do without her?*
> *My little helper is always happy to be in charge and help organise the other children.*

Don't we flipping well know it, always bossing us around and being Miss Superior.

Anyway, Botty was handing out rosettes all round, so I was LOOKING FORWARD to reading mine. It was probably going to be like: *We will never be able to thank Holly enough for saving the Christmas play this term. Holly was the hero of the day . . .*

I shall remember to blush and be all 'it was nothing' when Mum reads it out at home.

But, hang on a blinking minute, the start was not as expected . . .

> Holly is not a straightforward girl and one often feels that she is over-controlling. Holly needs to learn to be less dramatic and perhaps to take herself less seriously. It would also do her no harm to concentrate more on her work and less on OTHER people.

I could NOT believe my ears. You could have knocked me over with a baseball bat. Or even one of Harold's drumsticks. Bossy Bossom was giving me a right pasting.

And it didn't get any better – not that I'm going to **POISON** history by recording any more of her bile in MY memoirs.

HER report would be:

Bossy Bossom has had a difficult term. Her acting is very limited, but thanks to Holly she did have a BIG success with the lead part in our Christmas play, School of Rock.

But she is a bad cook and an even worse loser – her childish behaviour after the village cake-off was witnessed by the world. Miss Bossom needs to do better next term. And stop spending so much time mooning around Slinky Dave.

You see, ANYONE can chuck stuff into school reports.

But I now needed to correct my report; it was time for my **MAGIC POCKET WATCH** to spring into action.

When Miss Bossom got back from her coffee and biscuits, I managed to get her attention without getting mown down by the whiff of her breath.

The other kids were playing 'blindfold Vinnie'.

This is how it works:

They make him DIZZY by spinning him round and round and round; then he walks like the people in films who've drunk too much wine and falls over.

While the other kids think it's terrifically hilarious, I always get them to cut it out after about ten goes because I don't think it's good for Vinnie's progression in life.

But Vinnie was on his own today, as I had 'affairs of state' to deal with. Getting roasted in my school report is not good for Holly Hopkinson's upwardly sprouting business career. It could get leaked to any of my customers, thank you very much.

'EXCUSE YOU,'

I said to Miss Bossom in my 'cute' voice.

'BUT CAN YOU LOOK AT MY MAGIC POCKET WATCH, PLEASE?'

'HOW LOVELY,'

said Miss Bossom.

'WHEREVER DID YOU GET IT?'

'LOOK AT MY WATCH AND
LISTEN TO ME,'

I instructed, not getting tricked into chitchat.

'SPIRO, SPERO, SQUIGGLEOUS SCOTCH,
CAST YOUR EYES WHITHER MY WATCH.'

I said this three times nice and slowly, while I
waved my watch backwards and forwards, forwards
and backwards, in front of her nose.

It seemed to do the trick as
she went quite GOGGLE-EYED.

16

'MISS BOSSOM, YOU **WILL** REWRITE **MY** SCHOOL REPORT.'

'YES, HOLLY.'

'AND **YOU WILL MAKE IT**–'

But before I could finish my sentence, guess who came crashing through the doors into the classroom like a bull in a Chinese shop?

– YES. –

Vinnie, of course, the lunatic. Followed by my moose-terical* classmates.

'Children, please,' squawked Miss Bossom in her 'I've just been woken up in the middle of the night by a herd of giraffes crashing through my bedroom' voice.

So I had to bring my **MAGIC POCKET WATCH** session to a close **PROMPTO**, as they say in Burkina Faso.

> * MOOSE-TERICAL –
> behaviour only found
> in kids in the Chipping
> Topley area.

CHAPTER 1A

HISTORY'S LITTER BIN

WHEN I GOT BACK TO THE FARM, I
THOUGHT ABOUT STEAMING OPEN MY
SCHOOL REPORT BEFORE DAD GOT BACK
FROM THE CHEQUERS AND MUM ARRIVED
BACK FROM BEING A GURU IN LONDON.

Not that I was worried – my report would be showering me with roses. After all, Miss Bossom HAD said she'd change it.

When Mum and Dad finally appeared, they made a **terrible fuss** about getting Grandpa, Harold, Harmony, Aunt Electra, Barkley, Moggy, and Beanstalk, of course, into the kitchen.

Aunt Electra made a stupid noise as if it was the beginning of a film and Mum said,

'BIG MOMENT . . .
HOLLY'S FIRST REPORT
FROM MISS BOSSOM.'

(My lawless school in London didn't bother with reports because most of the parents wouldn't read them.)

I got ready to blush and thank everyone, like they do at awards for films and best milking cows.

And then Mum started to read:

'Holly is not a straightforward girl . . . She seems to feel that she can get everyone to do what she wants them to do, when she wants them to do it. Including the teachers. Some would say she is a control freak.'

After all that I have done to stop that DOOFUS of a woman making a complete fool of herself with her contrapted* Christmas play. And now she double-crosses me. How ungrateful CAN you be?

She is going to be judged alongside all the worst people in the world when this volume of my memoirs is discovered: Donald Trump, Henry VIII, Bart Simpson, Joseph Stalin and Miss Bossy Bossom. All in the litter bin of history together.

Aunt Electra followed me up to my bedroom where I went to huff.

'It didn't work, Aunt Electra . . . It didn't work . . . my **MAGIC POCKET WATCH** has lost its power . . . I don't GIVE A STUFF about my school report . . .' Then I sniffled quite a lot . . .

Well, cried out loud, actually . . . It was a sort of cross between a bison and a cockerel type of noise.

---

* CONTRAPTED
– contrary (as in Mary, Mary).

'Hang on there,' Aunt Electra said in her 'calm' voice. Not one she uses very often. 'We've been through this before, Holly . . . What exactly did you try to get it to do?'

'Get Miss Big Botty Bossom to change my report, of course . . . and she did . . . She made it worse.'

'Of course she did,' Aunt Electra said, 'because you forgot the golden rule . . . Every time you use your **MAGIC POCKET WATCH**, it must be for *good* or for *fun* . . . and didgeridoo-ing your report was neither, Holly, was it? The magic powers of your watch are fine . . . You just need to be careful how you use it.'

So that was the bit I'd forgotten – using it for good or fun – but,

HANG ON A MINUTE,

it would have been good for ME if she'd given me a better report – it might be crucial when I'm trying to become prime minister.

Some polite servant will be poking around in my past and suddenly say, 'Look, she can't be prime minister . . . just read this report from Miss Bossom.'*

\ | | /

— **LATE NEWS** – I was lieing in bed**, thinking about what Aunt Electra had told me, when I suddenly heard a thump-thump noise from the attic. So I rolled over and hoped I was just imagining it. Then it got a bit louder.

I peeped out from under my blankets and there in the door way was a shadowy white figure.

'Your school report was very bad, Holly . . . and that makes Mabel very cross,' a spooky voice whispered.

My legs were shaking like they were going round in the tumble dryer. And I was about to shout out to Aunt Electra when Mabel said . . .

* So my future is now very compromised. I am damaged goods. Not to mention that an iPad feels further away than ever.

** LIEING IN BED – having a dream that isn't true.

22

'And you are going to have to give all your pocket money and your mobile phone to Harold and Harmony as your punishment.'

And then Harold and Harmony started laughing and ran off down the corridor thinking they were very funny.

THEY WILL GET IT WHEN I GROW UP AND MY MEMOIRS ARE PUBLISHED.

CHAPTER 2

BACK AT THE RANCH

NONE OF US ACTUALLY CALL GRANDPA'S FARM, WHICH WE HAD TO MOVE TO WHEN DAD LOST HIS JOB IN LONDON, THE RANCH. BUT I THINK THE INTERNATIONAL READERS OF MY MEMOIRS – WHO I WILL MEET THROUGH BUSINESS – WILL AGREE IT'S A RATHER GOOD NAME FOR THIS CHAPTER. THANK YOU VERY MUCH.

Quite a lot has happened since I sealed the first volume of my memoirs in a time capsule cake tin in Grandpa's farmyard (not giving any clues). But I hope someone flipping well finds it one day or I will never be a famous writer of the times like Samuel Pepys.

So here is the **BREAKING NEWS** –
Grandpa says there's a racehorse sale coming up
and we are GOING to it.

Vince (the farmer from the other side of the
village) says he knows how to train horses. Which,
quite frankly, comes as a surprise to me, because
Vince doesn't look anything like the trainers we
see on the TV. He hasn't even got one of those hats
that they get from trainer school.

So I'm not that happy about Vince muscling in
on what was meant to be my deal. And Vinnie,
his nephew, is meant to be the animal one in their
family, I THOUGHT.

And, while I'm on THAT family, Vinnie's
nan Vera is still on the scene. She is officially in
charge of washing Grandpa's pants (what's left
of them), and is very much UNOFFICIALLY his
'lady friend'. She also stalks him like a secret
service agent.

I can imagine **DAGGERS** coming out of her shoes when she clicks her heels together, just like in the films. She can probably vamoose into thin air too.

I would NOT want to be under the sort of scrutiny that Grandpa's under. She does NOT approve of: racehorses, owning pubs or watching daytime TV cookery programmes.

The **GOOD NEWS** is that Harold and Stickly have officially got a name for the band. The **BAD NEWS** is it's The Cool. Which is pretty uncool if you ask me – but so are Harold and Stickly.

When I told Harold he's a doofus, all he said was 'Events, dear boy, events.' Because that's all Harold EVER says to me – I wish Dad hadn't taught him that stupid expression – no one even knows what it means.

because I am small and incontinento*, I have found out that Harmony has been talking to Dad about playing at the Chequers again. That is meant to be MY department, THANK you very much.

She is meant to be writing the flipping songs. Stuff about dessert islands** and having no money and your mum running off with the Amazon driver and stuff like that – because that's what most TOP pop songs are about.

I need to introduce some blurred lines or this whole thing is going to get out of hand. One day my family is going to have to stop squeezing me out of stuff or I'm leaving – and they'll regret that.

Now you can see why I NEED to get an iPad – you just don't cut the cloth without one.

BAD NEWS – Mum has done such a good job on the gardeners' parties for the queen at Buckingham Palace that they don't need her to help out any more.

---

* INCONTINENTO – invisible and hard to control.

** DESSERT ISLANDS – hot places where you eat pudding.

> **MORE BAD NEWS** – *School of Rock* is SO SUCCESSFUL (and I think Mum should take some credit for that) they've decided they don't need anyone to manipulate the press. So HER people have been let go by THEIR people.

But Mum did have some **GOOD NEW NEWS**.

The PR company Mum works for has landed a big account* with Union Jack Porker's Happy English Pork Pies.

Mum says these Happy English Pork Pies are going to be a culinary revolution, which sounds like trouble, and that's why they'll need Mum. Because she is still a guru.

HEY, GIRL.
HOW GOES IT/EVERYTHING COOL?
LET'S GET TOGETHER.

* ACCOUNT – pretend-tious word for job.

Guess who sent me this text message this evening?

Someone who history thought had gone walkabout for good.

YES.

My ex-best friend, Aleeshaa, no doubt texting me from her dad's swish art gallery, Black Hebesphenomegacorona, in Notting Hill.

So what's brought that on, you might be thinking, seeing as I haven't heard from her for flipping donkey's years. She'd better have a Captain Scott double-whopper good explanation.

Anyway, I'm going to give her a cold front for a bit to teach her not to put Holly Hopkinson into the wilderness for forty months and forty days. I shall not be replying for some time –

TWO CAN PLAY TANGO!

CHAPTER 3

LAST DAY OF SCHOOL TERM

DAD DROPPED ME OFF AT SCHOOL ON HIS WAY TO THE CHEQUERS. HE WAS VERY STRESSED THAT HE WOULDN'T HAVE ENOUGH CUSTOMERS TODAY TO IMPRESS THE TV CREW WHO ARE COMING TO FILM AN EPISODE OF *STICK THAT IN YOUR OVEN*.

My MAGIC POCKET WATCH and I need to take some responsibility for his stress for TWO reasons.

1. It was my idea that Dad should become a world-famous TV celebrity chef, so he can sell squillions of cookbooks.

2. It was ALSO my idea that he create some EXOTIC dishes to photograph for what Mum calls 'those ridiculous books' . . . but they are causing him SLEEPLESS nights.

So I need to help him out, DOUBLE-WHOPPER quick time. I DO NOT like seeing my dad with his knicks in a twist.

Anyway, Slinky Dave, the school bus driver, was hanging about polishing bits of the bus that didn't need polishing. And I had a GOOD idea.

'LOOK AT MY MAGIC POCKET WATCH,'

I said.

'THAT LOOKS NICE,' he remarked innocently.

'SPIRO, SPERO, SQUIGGLEOUS SCOTCH,
CAST YOUR EYES WHITHER MY WATCH.'

I said to Dave for two verses.

I was confident this would work – because it is GOOD for Dad if people turn up to his pub. So it really couldn't go codswallop wrong THIS time.

'Dave . . . can you go to the coach station in Chipping Topley and tell all the drivers to take their passengers to the Chequers for lunch, please?' I requested.

'THAT MIGHT BE QUITE A LOT OF PEOPLE,'

he warned.

'LEAVE THE WORRYING TO ME, DAVE,'

I replied.

'THE MORE, THE MERRIER.'

32

○○○

The last day at school is a real swizz; hardly anyone turns up. You should hear the excuses that are trotted out. I must have been asleep when the hurricane carrying **BUBONIC PLAGUE** blew through the village last night.

☆ **WOLFE** – sick bug (gone skiing)

☆ **TIGER** – temperature (gone to Disneyland)

☆ **IRIS** – cough (gone Christmas shopping)

☆ **GASPAR** – earache (probably gone to visit the wise men in Bethlehem for all I know)

☆ **CROCUS** – tummy ache (gone to Water World)

☆ **FELICITY SNOOP** – sore throat (riding her pony, more like it)

☆ **VINNIE** – he just didn't turn up . . .

So there I was, sitting like a lemon with Daffodil, making decorations for a Christmas tree. Thank YOU very much.

After the report I copped from Bossy, I deliberately left her Christmas present from Mum at home. Although I was TEMPTED to give it to her because Mum had got her skintight leggings, for goodness' sake.

If Botty Bossom had got them on, she'd have spent Christmas in Accident and Incident, waiting ten hours to have them surgically removed. I don't know what goes through my mother's head sometimes.

But at least being at school gave me the chance to make some holiday plans with my OFFICIAL best friend Daffodil, while she glued her fingers together trying to make an angel.

'How about coming round to the den on the farm tomorrow?' I asked. 'I have a new selection of biscuits that happen to have come my way – no questions asked.'

It was what Dad calls a rheumatoidical* question because she loves coming and hanging out with me and Vinnie in our secret Bogey Club** den.

But, blow me down with a hurricane-carrying **BUBONIC PLAGUE**, she said, 'I'm afraid I can't tomorrow . . . I'm having a riding lesson at Felicity Snoop's house.'

NO . . . NO . . . NO . . . NO . . . **NOOOO!**

Now I am the only girl in my class who doesn't ride. And this is a deliberate ploy by 'the little helper' Felicity Snoop to win back Daffodil as her best friend.

'Excuse you,' I said to Daffodil. 'Can I come too and share your pony . . .¿ I'd love to learn to ride.'

'I don't think Felicity would like that,' Daffodil replied curtly.

'WOULDN'T LIKE WHAT?'

* RHEUMATOIDICAL –
disorderly question that
doesn't have an answer.

** BOGEY CLUB – see
Volume I.

'Well, you coming too . . . I don't think she likes you.'

If that isn't a slap in the face with a bit of wet cod, I DO NOT KNOW WHAT IS.

THIS IS A **DISASTROUS** END

TO MY FIRST TERM.

THIS WOULD NOT HAVE HAPPENED IF WE WERE STILL IN LONDON.

So, on the way home from school to the farm, I decided to pack my bags and head back to London.

CHAPTER 4

THE SPIRIT OF GRANDMA ESME

'FEEL LIKE A CHAT?'

AUNT ELECTRA ASKED AS SHE POKED
HER HEAD ROUND MY BEDROOM DOOR
(CATCHING ME PACKING). IT WAS ANOTHER
RHEUMATOIDICAL QUESTION
BECAUSE BEFORE I COULD SAY 'NOT
RIGHT NOW ACTUALLY', SHE
WAS COSYING UP TO ME ON MY BED,
SMELLING OF **MARSHMALLOWS** AND
CANDYFLOSS – WHICH I LIKE.

So I decided to shoot the breeze with her.

'I haven't got any friends . . . Aleeshaa has
abandoned me and none of the country children
like me . . . apart from Vinnie . . . but he's
part animal.'

'Now that isn't true,' Aunt Electra said softly. 'It's just difficult when you have to move . . . The same happened to me when we left New York with Grandpa.'

'About New York, Aunt Electra . . . why were you actually there?'

'Well, Grandpa used to paint there.'

'PAINT . . . WHAT, LIKE BUILDINGS . . . WAS GRANDPA A DECORATOR?'

'No, silly . . . He was trying to be an artist most of the time . . . He was part of the abstract expressionist movement . . . and he was friends with some of the great painters . . . Jackson Pollock . . . Mark Rothko . . . but HE never sold any paintings . . . That's why we came home.'

'So he hasn't really been a farmer in Little Goring all his life?'

'Good lord, no . . . Pa doesn't know anything about farming . . . This is just where he ended up.'

Well, flipping **DOUBLE-WHOPPER** blow me down with a feather; I've always had a doubt about Grandpa and his farming carry-on.

'Anyway, Holly . . . I know what you're going through . . . and you just have to stick at it, my darling girl . . . and keep using your **MAGIC POCKET WATCH** . . . and it will all be OK in the end.'

'BUT I KEEP **MESSING UP WITH IT**.'

'Well, I'm sure you'll work that out too.'

'Aunt Electra . . . you know you said you got it from Grandma Esme . . . well, who gave it to her?'

'Well, that's a very interesting question . . . You see, Esme's mother was called Constance, and she had a rather difficult life . . . but she was very, very good at tennis.'

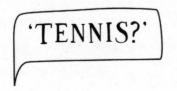

'TENNIS?'

'Yes . . . so good, in fact, that she was Prime Minister Stanley Baldwin's tennis coach. And in 1928 she HYPNOTISED the prime minister while she was working on his forehand and told him to pass a bill in Parliament giving equal voting rights to women. Which was very GOOD for women.'

Hmm . . . some of my history textbooks must have got this wrong.

Then Aunt Electra gave me a WET KISS on my cheek and I had to refrain from wiping it off before she went back downstairs.

But Aunt Electra has pulled me back from the brink. Holly Hopkinson is going to TOUGH THIS OUT.

CHAPTER 4A

CHAOS AT THE CHEQUERS

BUT IN MY **DARK** CLOUD OF **TURMOIL** AND **GLOOM** I'D COMPLETELY FORGOTTEN ABOUT DAD'S DAY – AND SLINKY DAVE'S MISSION.

Alarm bells started flashing when I went downstairs. Grandpa was bouncing around the kitchen like he'd been at the icing sugar all afternoon.

'Have you heard . . .⸮ The Chequers was chaos this afternoon . . . complete **DISASTER** . . . Coachloads of people trying to get some grub . . . the TV presenter said it was the **worst-run pub** he'd **ever** been to.'

'Coaches . . . from the coach station⸮' I asked.

'OH.'

41

Then Dad arrived back, looking like he'd had his fingers stuck in an **ELECTRIC** socket all afternoon.

'Everything OK, Dad?' I asked.

'Don't ask,' he huffed. 'I was cooking Turnip Scallopini with Pomegranate Seeds à la Plancha for *Stick That in Your Oven* when half of the world's population turned up . . . Some **MANIAC** at the coach station told them we served lunch all afternoon . . . and only me and Vinnie were there.'

'Vinnie?' I said, my ears twitching like an agitated Martian. 'Excuse you, but what was Vinnie doing there . . . ? He was meant to be at school making Christmas decorations with me.'

'Vinnie's got a job washing up in the Chequers,' piped up Vera from nowhere, rather too smugly for my liking.

This is a double-whopper disaster. Not only have I added to Dad's stress, but another of my **MAGIC POCKET WATCH** hypnotic ventures has gone pear-shaped on me. That's two in a row, thank you very much.

CHAPTER 5

ANOTHER FARM

MORE NEWS ARRIVED FOR MUM
WHEN SHE GOT BACK FROM LONDON –
FROM HARMONY OF ALL PEOPLE.

I happened to be behind the sofa, not minding my own beeswax, when Harmony started quizzing Mum like it was one of those undercover TV shows.

'Mum . . . like, why are they called Union Jack Porker's Happy English Pork Pies? They sooo aren't.'

'Because they're made at Happy Farm with one hundred per cent English ingredients,' Mum replied in her 'official PR' voice.

'But, Mum . . . they're sooo not . . . Like . . . have you been to Happy Farm?'

She knows jolly well that Mum has only been to one farm in her life – the one we're flipping well living on.

'Well, I've seen pictures of it,' Mum replied defensively.

'Like, really . . . it's sooo not OK . . . It's in an industrial park in the docks in east London,' Harmony responded defiantly.

Mum wasn't expecting that one judging by the 'really BAD smell' look on her face.

'Well, I'm not quite sure exactly where it is.'

'Or maybe you're, like, getting SOOO confused with the industrial sheds where most of the meat actually comes from,' continued Harmony.

'Don't be silly, Harmony . . . They're English pies.'

'No, Mum . . . The meat is sooo not produced in England . . . That's why we're sooo, like, going to protest outside Happy Farm.'

'OH, SHIPS,' said Mum glumly.

While Mum was cooking supper (not pies), Harmony took me upstairs to her bedroom and we did some poking around on the internet.

It isn't looking good for Union Jack Porker's Happy English Pork Pies. If you read the small print – which is so small you need the Hubble Space Telescope to read it – the only English bit about the pies is that all the ingredients are squished into them in east London.

Mum could end up in deep doo-doo if she so much as sniffs one of these pies.

If Aleeshaa comes to stay at the farm, it will show Daffodil Chichester that I have other official best friend options.

So my texting fingers got busy. It was time to get Aleeshaa off the cold bench.

> HEY, ALEESHAA – JUST PICKED UP YOUR MESSAGE. **REALLY BUSY** WITH MY BAND AND STUFF – YOU KNOW HOW IT IS. WHY DON'T YOU COME DOWN HERE TO CHILL AND WATCH A GIG? XX

She will be blown away by me having a band – just so long as she doesn't hear them.

CHAPTER 6

THE HORSE SALE

AFTER LESS SLEEP THAN A TEACUP IN A
STORM - MORE FLIPPING OWLS HOOTING
AND PARTYING ALL NIGHT, THANK YOU
VERY MUCH - I STILL WOKE UP EARLY.

It was time to set Mum on the right path with
a little bit of help from my **MAGIC POCKET
WATCH**. That, after all, is what you have youngest
children for.

I found her in the kitchen stuffing down some
mushed avocado and chilli before computing to
London to see HER people.

'D'you like my **MAGIC POCKET WATCH**, Mum?' I asked, wiggling it in front of her mush.

'Very nice, Holly, but I must rush. Can you feed the chickens?'

So I did three verses in **DOUBLE-WHOPPER** quick time before she could bolt out of the door.

'SPIRO, SPERO, SQUIGGLEOUS SCOTCH, CAST YOUR EYES WHITHER MY WATCH.'

I repeated three times.

'Mum, will you do something for me?' I asked once I saw she was **GOGGLE-EYED**.

'Of course, Holly, at your service.'

'Good . . . so when you see YOUR people this morning, you're going to tell them that you are NOT going to work on the Union Jack Porker's Happy English Pork Pies account . . .

There is nothing happy or English about these pies
. . . They are piglets in wolves' clothing.'

'ARE YOU SURE?'

'CERTAIN, MUM.'

'Well, if you say so . . . Now, I'd better rush for the train or I won't be seeing anyone today.'

Whether my **MAGIC POCKET WATCH** had worked I just couldn't say for sure. Anyway, Grandpa and I had bigger fish to fry today – we were off to the racehorse sale. Of course we're taking Vinnie with us because he can possibly talk to horses if they can understand what he's saying. But that is a big IF.

Horse sales are like being in a different world. To start with it's very hard to understand what anyone says, because they all speak out of the side of their mouths.

The man selling the first horse we looked at said his horse came from Tipperary in Ireland, adding, 'To be sure, this fella's going to be a champion.'

49

So that was a bit of luck. Finding out that the first flipping horse you looked at was the one who was going to be a champion.

'He's one for you, young lady . . . He'll run through a wall for you,' the man said out of the side of his mouth. But as Vinnie, our official interpreter and communications SUPREMO had vamoosed, I decided to take matters into my own hands.

So I slipped into the stable and got my **MAGIC POCKET WATCH** out. I just hoped it would work on racehorses from Ireland like it did with Beanstalk on the farm.

'SPIRO, SPERO, SQUIGGLEOUS SCOTCH, CAST YOUR EYES WHITHER MY WATCH.'

I repeated five times to the horse.

'Do you want to be a racehorse . . .? Will you "run through a wall" for me?' I asked in a horsey-sounding voice.

Well, he just looked at me with a bored expression and tried to bite me. And he nearly got hold of my flipping watch – that was a CLOSE SHAVE.

Imagine having to buy a horse because he'd swallowed my watch – and then having to go through his doings for the next few days until it came out the other end, for goodness' sake.

But eating a MAGIC POCKET WATCH is not the attitude of a champion, thank you very much.

'Hey, buster,' I told the shifty dealer out of the corner of my mouth. 'You picked the wrong person to play games with . . . We know our onions from our strawberries . . . so good day to you, sir.'

You see, that's how you have to deal with horse dealers – it's all they understand.

Anyway, before I could find another future champion to try my MAGIC POCKET WATCH on, Vinnie came bustling round the corner.

'Yer man, I have one for yer,' he said to Grandpa.

'Don't you start with this weird talking, Vinnie,' I said. 'We can't understand half of what you say in English, let alone horse speak.'

Vinnie had been mooching around with some horses out the back of the sale ring and he said he'd found a big brown one that was mustard keen to be a top racehorse. As long as he's fed a LOT and given stuff that normal horses don't get.

''E's a diamond, so he is,' Vinnie muttered in his new language. And, as it turned out, his dad is by Royal Approval, just like Fist Bump and High Five. (If you don't know who they are, you're reading the wrong book by the way.)

So I was about to go and do my interrogation with my **MAGIC POCKET WATCH** when Grandpa told me we had to lie low.

Apparently at horse sales you have to be **DEAD COOL** and pretend you don't like anything. But guess who Grandpa decided should do the bidding for the nag?

YES.

Me – the official racing manager.

I've seen people bidding for things at auctions on low-budget TV shows and it's a right carry-on. There are two ways you can do it, plus one more.

---

1. Look as poor as possible and then everyone feels sorry for you and lets you win.

2. Look as rich as possible and then everyone gives up because they think you have **more** money than them.

OR

3. Look like a cute little girl and start sniffling and boohooing so the adults have to stop bidding to shut you up.

Well, I put on a right display – you've never seen anything like it. After a few bids I started stamping my feet just like Harmony does when she doesn't get her way and in the end all the adults ducked for cover and, BOB'S YOUR UNCLE, I had the winning bid.

Then, just as we were about to leave, I saw this titchy racehorse being led around with no one taking any notice of it – and I had a 'hey pesto' bolt-from-Damascus moment*.

'Vinnie, why don't you go and have one of your chats with that little fellow over there?' I suggested.

Vinnie shook his head with a look of **HORROR**. 'Too small for nothing,' he garbled.

'Not to be a racehorse, you mutt . . . For me to beat Felicity Snoop on . . . Go on, have a chat with him.'

'ALL RIIGHT.'

The reluctant Vinnie sloped up to the miniscule racehorse and had a chinwag.

''E's interested in meeting you . . . 'E's name's Declan,' Vinnie reported back.

* 'HEY PESTO' BOLT-FROM-DAMASCUS MOMENT – way too difficult to explain.

Introductions served, my **MAGIC POCKET WATCH** and I slipped behind the barn with Declan, and after a couple of verses of Spiro, Spero, I put Declan on the spot.

'If you will help me beat Felicity Snoop and her orbiting flowers on their ponies, please nod, Declan,' I said.

Declan looked a little nervous but he nodded enthusiastically – I suppose it was probably the ONLY offer he was going to get all day.

So after the briefest negotiation with Declan's owner – during which I had to dismiss quite forcefully his belief that Declan was going to be the SECOND champion I had met that day – we triumphantly took Declan and Vinnie's 'diamond' (don't worry, we're not going to call him that) back to Lower Goring.

SO WE ARE NOW BACK IN THE RACEHORSE BUSINESS – EVEN IF ONE OF THEM HAS BEEN SHRUNK.

CHAPTER 7

MUM GETS FIRED

MUM WAS HOME EARLY WHEN WE GOT BACK FROM THE HORSE SALE, WHICH WAS A NICE SURPRISE – BUT NOT FOR LONG.

She was looking as white as a GOAT.

'I don't know what came over me,' she said. 'I walked into the office this morning and told MY people we shouldn't promote Union Jack Porker's Happy English Pork Pies . . . and they sacked me . . . I've lost MY JOB.'

'But I thought they were YOUR people, Mum?' I pointed out.

'Well, they're not any more,' said Aunt Electra.

'What made you say that?' Dad asked. 'They were going to pay you a FORTUNE!'

'I think it must have been something Harmony said last night,' Mum said.

I made a noise like air coming out of a balloon as it flies around the room. But luckily no one noticed.

What the flipping heck is my **MAGIC POCKET WATCH** up to? The Hopkinson family is now facing a famine of money and food again – even though we own a flipping pub.

'Yes, Harmony was going on about the pies,' I said, crossing my fingers behind my back.

Thank goodness my 'revolting'* sister wasn't there to clear her name – that was a stroke of luck.

Poor Mum – THIS IS A **DISASTER**

AND IT'S ALL **MY FAULT!**

Mum was not feeling very guru-ish, but the world keeps spinning and we were due at the VCEOC meeting (I do the biscuits and sweeping up as part of my voluntary and espionage work).

> * REVOLTING – protesting revolting, as opposed to Vera's cooking revolting.

'I'm sorry about your job, Mum,' I said on our way to the meeting. 'Is there any way it could be for the good?'

'I don't think so – I really liked that job,' Mum whimpered.

THIS IS A **TERRIBLE** DAY FOR HOLLY HOPKINSON!

There was an air of expectation in the village hall. Mrs Smartside, the automatic* chairperson, was full of agendas and self-importance as I handed round the biscuits.

'Hush, everyone . . . some decorum, PLEASE . . . We shall be organising the following events over the Christmas period.'

'Item One . . . the Christmas Nativity Duck Race . . . Charmian, I believe you are *chef d'équipe* of the plastic ducks.'

* AUTOMATIC –
immediately
assumes control.

58

Charmian is none other than Charmian Chichester, Daffodil's mother. She is Chipping Topley's worst and only interior decorator (according to Dad). She was also in charge of the ducks at the village fete and she made a right mess of that.

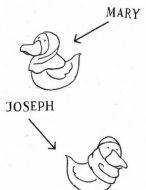

MARY

JOSEPH

'We shall name all the ducks after characters in the Nativity scenes: Mary, Joseph, Baby Jesus, et cetera . . . and float them down the river from the village hall to the church . . .'

BABY JESUS

Mrs Chichester explained. 'Let's just hope King Herod doesn't sink them all,' she tittered. 'Anyone who buys a ticket can own the winning duck.'

Because I'm meant to be invisibly sweeping up and handing round biscuits, I am not allowed to be seen or heard. But I was bursting to put my hand up and point out why that is all rubbish.

1. Jesus hasn't been born on Christmas Eve, so how can he be floating down the river to the church?

2. Her timing is DOUBLE-WHOPPER wrong with King Herod – she's worse at history than Bossy Bossom.

'Well done, Charmian,' said Mrs Smartside, oblivious to the historical clangers. 'Item Two . . . the children's and dogs' fancy dress show . . . Sally dear, I think that's your department.'

'Sally dear' is Mum.

'Well, I thought the children and dogs could all dress up in festive outfits . . .' Mum said. And then her voice sort of petered out.

'What about people who don't have dogs?' asked Vera in her 'Northern' voice.

'THEY COULD BRING THEIR CAT INSTEAD?' suggested Mum.

It was time for me to take Mum home. It had been a long day.

'Yee-es, Sally . . . well, maybe that one needs a bit more thought?' Mrs Smartside advised. 'Item Three . . . the Yuletide Log Competition . . . Has anyone seen Vincent?'

'He's not here,' said Vera.

'I can see that, thank you, Vera . . . Well, where is he . . .? He's meant to be briefing us on what size the logs will be this year . . . Vicar, can you PLEASE touch base with Vincent and sort this out?'

Our vicar has chosen the VCEOC meeting to give a run out to one of his Caribbean-themed shirts, which was not tucked in, in a 'cool' sort of way. He looked quite **RIDICULOUS**.

'Item Four . . . the village pony show . . . Charmian?'

My heart started racing – no one had told ME there was going to be an Xmas pony show.

'Well, we're going to go with an Xmas theme,' Mrs Chichester said in her big-cheese 'interior design' voice.

'You're not kidding – at Christmas – well, blow my socks off,' I nearly said.

'The first class will be a bending race at the walk for health-and-safety reasons . . . with a best-dressed prize for Pony Club members in the correct tie . . . sponsored by Chichester Fabrics.'

Is Holly Hopkinson the only person who can see that the Chichesters are making a takeover bid for pony stuff?

'Then we're going to have a dressing-up extravaganza . . . Children as Santa and their ponies as reindeers . . . sponsored by Chichester Interior Design.'

I wonder who the genius was who came up with that one?

And on she went . . .
                    and on . . .
                                and on.

'Perhaps Sally could do some PR for the pony show?' Mrs Smartside suggested.

'SORRY?'

said Mum, who wasn't taking much in.

'Could you do some PR for the pony show?' Mrs Smartside said in her 'slow and rather deliberate' voice that she uses for people like Vinnie.

'Yes . . . of course . . . I can be on the Pony Club committee if you like?'

'Well, that won't be necessary, Sally. Perhaps you could just be affiliated to the Pony Club committee,' said Mrs Chichester sharply, ready to defend her newly won territory like it was the Siege of Leningrad.

So that was the second slap in the face with a bit of wet haddock that Mum had had in one day.

Finally they had a quick vote on getting Bossy Bossom to run a village quiz night and then Mum and I were able to spit-spot back to the farm.

Mum took herself off to bed as soon as we got home so she missed the *LATE NEWS*.

Aunt Electra has officially been appointed general manager of the Chequers after the bus crisis. She is now in charge of all non-food matters, such as entertainment and coaches. And, given that she had just landed such a big job, I was touched that she spent some time putting me to bed – and chatting to me about the top-secret VCEOC meeting.

We had a terrific GIGGLE about Mum telling everyone they could bring their cat to dress up if they didn't have a dog. And she wanted to know all about the Pony Club show.

That's Aunt Electra for you – she's always got time for others, and she knows what I'm up against.

Aleeshaa texted me:

HEY, GIRL – JUST SO SUPER BUSY WITH THE NEW EXHIBITION COMING UP IN DAD'S GALLERY. WILL MAKE IT OUT TO YOU SOON.

I'll give her 'hey, girl' when I see her.

CHAPTER 8

THE COOL

EARLY NEWS -

NO SIGN OF MUM THIS MORNING ANYWHERE
OUTSIDE HER BEDROOM. SO I AM WALKING
AROUND IN A CLOUD OF DENSE DOOM,
BECAUSE ME AND MY MAGIC POCKET
WATCH HAVE COST MUM HER JOB.

I wonder if Aunt Electra giving me this magic watch wasn't one big trick?

The reason my brother Harold slips in and out of these memoirs is because he lives in a parallel universe that oscillates between his scratcher and the cowshed where his 'recording studio' is. Although it doesn't have any recording equipment in it yet.

65

That would be putting the horse before the cart because they haven't got any good songs – in fact, they haven't even got a full band. It's only Harold and Stickly at the moment.

> But here is the **BAND NEWS** – Harold and Stickly are auditing* today – and hopefuls will be turning up at hourly intervals to see if they can join. So I'm going to keep an eye on that.

The first bloke was called Hedge. He is a singer – or maybe was a singer, because he defo isn't any more from what I heard through the back window.

What a racket. The chickens scarpered all over the place, jetting stuff out as they went,

THANK you

very much.

Even Harold could spot that he was a dud. As were the next two . . . but then they struck **GOLD**.

* AUDITING – counting band hopefuls.

66

The coolest chick you've ever seen showed up . . .

She walked into the farmyard
Like she was walking on to a yacht
Her hat strategically dipped below one eye
Her scarf smelled of apricot.

Maybe I should be writing the songs for this band? Although Charly Simon might come after me when he reads that verse, because it is a bit like the one he did.

Harold and Stickly's ears started twitching as soon as they saw Badger's long blonde hair flowing through the door and her cute freckles. But, weirdly, Harmony wasn't blown away by her at all.

She says her voice was flat, although it sounded pretty good to

ME!

Anyway, Harold and Stickly overruled Harmony and I got Badger's signature on a contract, thank you **very** much. The Cool are now **OFFICIALLY** fully formed and ready for some gigs.

So, with my business pants on, I went straight to the top and offered Aunt Electra and the Chequers exclusive rights for their first tour.

But Aunt Electra asked if any of them could play the violin. What sort of question is that? I don't suppose gig location managers went round asking Adele if she could play the violin when she was bursting on to the scene.

You see, Aunt Electra is a bit inexperienced with music matters. Then she muttered, 'Hmmm . . . she's going to be trouble,' when she saw Badger.

Badger doesn't look in the slightest bit like she'd ever be in trouble – in fact, I think she's

♡   DOUBLE-WHOPPER   ♡   ♡
♡   ♡   lovely.   ♡

And she is very nice to me. So I think Aunt Electra's way off the pitch with that one.

But my main priority as band manager right now is lack of housing, because Stickly's family are about to be booted out of the house they rent. These are the sort of things band managers have to sort out. It's not all velvet carpets and slap-up lunches, pardon my French.

I managed to find some time during my back-to-back meetings to send Aleeshaa a text.

YEAH, FULL ON DOWN HERE TOO. JUST SIGNED UP A NEW MEMBER OF THE BAND SO UP TO MY EARS IN CONTRACTS – ORGANISING GIGS AND STUFF LIKE THAT. THESE VENUES ARE A NIGHTMARE. ANYWAY, LET ME KNOW WHEN YOU'RE PASSING.

LUNCHTIME NEWS – I'm beginning to think that my relationship with Vinnie has become a bit distant. Of course I'm busy with my new business commitments, but it's mainly his fault because:

1. He is spending a lot of time in the Chequers, washing up.

2. He is spending a lot of time with Grandpa's new horses.

Anyway, I dropped into the Chequers before lunch – NOT to see Vinnie; I just wanted to check out where The Cool will play to stop people in the bar talking over them (like last time).

So here is the **KITCHEN NEWS** – there was no sign of Dad and they've got twenty people booked in for a bistro lunch. So guess who is cooking lunch? None other than the phantom cake baker of Chipping Topley town cum Little Goring village.

YUP. Vera the destroyer.

If word gets out that she is anywhere near that kitchen, the Chequers will be doomed – they'll be queuing up from everywhere to not come here.

This time Dad's gone to London to be on a show called *You Won't Believe Who's Cooking Our Dinner Tonight!* Which makes me wonder who makes up these ridiculous names for cooking shows? Because I think I could do better:

You see . . .
it's not difficult.

71

MUM didn't get out of bed today – she didn't even leave her bedroom. Except to snitch a packet of digested biscuits from the store cupboard when no one was around. I know that because I was planning on having a few for my tea.

Even Grandpa has vamoosed. He normally covers my back when everyone else scatters, but he's gone to see his new horses. I shall join him tomorrow.

As I suspected, my mention of gigs seems to have freed up Aleeshaa's diary, as they say in Hollywood. It would appear she's found a gap between exhibitions to make it down to Little Goring.

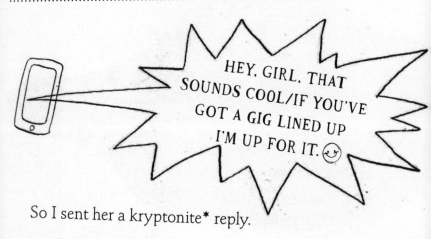

HEY, GIRL, THAT SOUNDS COOL/IF YOU'VE GOT A GIG LINED UP I'M UP FOR IT.

So I sent her a kryptonite* reply.

 xx

* KRYPTONITE –
confusing reply that is very hard to understand.

CHAPTER 9

THE CHEQUERS XMAS ENTERTAINMENTS CALENDAR

> **HORSE NEWS** –
>
> GRANDPA HAS CALLED HIS NEW HORSE LE PRINCE. HE SAYS HE MIGHT BE ABLE TO SELL THIS ONE TO THE QUEEN TOO.

As planned, I went with Grandpa to see Le Prince up at Vince's farm this morning. He's living in a very big stable with a lot of straw in it. He also has a sheep called Billy who keeps him company and a very nice lady who brushes and feeds him.

Declan has a very small stable and a chicken called Chicken to keep him company. It was standing on his back when we arrived.

I couldn't help but notice that when Grandpa looked at the lady brushing Le Prince, he went a bit BOGGLE-EYED.

Vince, Grandpa and I had a good chat leaning over the gate and chewing grass, like you do in the countryside.

You can see the village from Vince's gate – in fact, you can even make out Mrs Smartside's washing line – which gave me a GOOD idea. Where better for Stickly's family to have a house?

So I got out my MAGIC POCKET WATCH and waved it in front of Vince's nose. I decided not to muck about and gave him five verses to make double-whopper sure that he was 'cooked'.

'SPIRO, SPERO, SQUIGGLEOUS SCOTCH,
CAST YOUR EYES WHITHER MY WATCH.'

'Vince, it would be a good idea if you were to build a house for Stickly's family in your field,' I commanded. 'Nice and close to the village . . . over there next to Mrs Smartside's garden.'

 'AH, HOLLY,' Vince agreed.

'How long will it take you?' I asked, spitting out my grass, which hadn't been the tastiest I'd ever chewed. I might not even have been the first animal to have had a chew on it.

'I'll put in for planning permission right away,' Vince grunted.

EXCELLENT.

Job done, problem solved. That's how you get on in business. You have to think with your feet.

Grandpa took me to the Chequers for a spot of lunch on the way back. Dad was still absent but Aunt Electra was there, being important and generally managing things. And while we were having our nosh-up, she unveiled the OFFICIAL Chequers Xmas Entertainments Calendar.

All the media had been invited to this
GRAND UNVEILING. Even the bloke
from the *Daily Chipping Topley Mail*, plus a woman
from RoundaboutChippingTopley.com.

There was a quite terrific uptake of the free
booze offer while the events were being announced.

Sir Garfield, Dad's butcher friend, seemed
DOUBLE-WHOPPER particularly keen to make sure
he didn't miss any of the announcements.

But guess who were conspicuous by the fact that
everyone would have noticed that they were there
if they had been but they weren't?

YES.

Mrs Smartside and Charmian Chichester.

I'll tell you who did turn up, though, looking
all snuggly and BOGGLE-EYED – Miss Bossom and
Slinky Dave.

One day they're going to get caught by headmistress Miss Growler and then they will both be up to their neck in it.

I can just hear it. 'As headmistress, I do not approve of snuggling and BOGGLE-EYEING.'

'Sorry, Miss Growler, we were just checking the back of the bus for textbooks,' Slinky Dave will say in his 'we've been busted' voice.

But I'm getting distracted. The FIRST event to be unveiled is the Road to Bethlehem Shepherds' and Wisemen's Duck Race.

It's down the river from the bridge above the church past the ruined Lower Goring Hall (still empty and apparently haunted) to the Chequers.

And THAT sounds distinctly familiar to someone else's duck race…

The next event unveiled is the Festive Fancy Dress Party for Cats and Children. And Aunt Electra was at pains to report OFFICIALLY that if you haven't got a cat, you can bring a dog. That sounded a bit familiar as well!!

By this stage the free drinks were going down well and noise levels were getting out of hand, so Vinnie had to bang a few glasses together.

'Our third event will be the inaugural running of the Chequers Xmas Pony Race,' Aunt Electra declared.

Well, that one really did send my ears twirling around the top of my head.

A pony race?

'And, finally, we shall be holding the traditional Chequers Xmas pub quiz, made up by none other than Miss Bossom.'

Fancy getting Lower Goring's least-talented schoolmistress to make up the pub quiz? Aunt Electra might as well have asked Vinnie to knock one up.

Anyway, Aunt Electra put on a pretty good show, although I did point out to her that having The Cool playing would have 'bigged' the whole thing up. But she is a bit inexperienced in that department.

HOWEVER,
IT WAS NOW DAWNING ON ME
WHERE AUNT ELECTRA HAD GOT
HER IDEAS FROM.

OFFICIAL DENIAL –
I am denying ever mentioning anything to Aunt Electra about the VCEOC meeting. So even if someone starts pulling my fingernails out or sticking Vince's blowtorch near my toes, they will get nothing from me. What are adults like?

Mum was still in her bedroom when I got home so I took her a cup of tea – I was going to take her a biscuit too, but the other packet has vamoosed. Either Mum or Mabel has been very hungry.

Mum was tucked under her sheets like the wolf in Little Red Riding Hood – and for a minute I thought, *Just my luck – I'm going to be eaten.*

But thankfully it WAS Mum.

She was still not looking too chipper, so I decided that it was time to give her a boost.

'Mum, you are going to spring into action like the guru that you are and do lots of important things,' I told her while I swung my MAGIC POCKET WATCH forwards and backwards, backwards and forwards, reciting my SPIRO, SPERO chant three times.

'Starting with coming downstairs now to watch Dad on *You Won't Believe Who's Cooking Our Dinner Tonight?* on TV.'

'Yes, Holly,' Mum said with a smile on her face for the first time since she had got back from London.

I
LOVE
MY MUM.

Grandpa, Vera, Aunt Electra, Vinnie, Harmony, Harold, Barkley, Moggy and Beanstalk were all gathered round the TV waiting for Dad to come on. Beanstalk had to budge up a bit because she's got a big bum for a small pony.

Who would the celebrity be that Dad was cooking for?

It was VERY exciting . . . until the programme started.

As this is a serious historical memoir I am NOT going to besmirch it with the name of the so-called celebrity.

Celebrities are meant to be famous. Since when did kicking a football around for a team that never wins anything and falling out of nightclubs qualify anyone to be called famous, thank you very much?

And it obviously does not make them grateful when they have a nice plate of Turnip Scallopini with Pomegranate Seeds à la Plancha plonked in front of them.

Poor Dad didn't know where to throttle himself when the ball-kicking person scraped it into the bin.

THIS IS ALL MY FAULT –
I WAS THE ONE WHO TOLD DAD
TO BE A CELEBRITY CHEF –
I WILL HAVE TO DO SOMETHING.

— **MEDICAL NEWS** —

I had a quiet word with Aunt Electra to see if she thinks I can reverse my 'you will become a TV celebrity chef' **MAGIC POCKET WATCH** hypnotism of Dad, but she doesn't think I can.

My **MAGIC** IS NOT helping my parents. Perhaps a **DARK** spell has been cast over me?

CHAPTER 9A

ALEESHAA'S GRAND VISIT

ALEESHAA IS COMING FOR A NIGHT STAY-
OVER. THIS IS A TERRIFIC OPPORTUNITY
TO STICK ONE ON DAFFODIL IN THE BEST
FRIEND DEPARTMENT AND SHOW HER
THAT I HAVE NOTTING HILL CONNECTIONS.

Dad took me to Chipping Topley station to meet
her. I'd been thinking about the platform reunion
scene all morning.

As the train chugged out of the station it would
just be me and Aleeshaa standing there as the steam
cleared. She would probably drop her suitcases and
come running up to give me a hug.

As it happened Aleeshaa was busy on her phone
when she got off the train, just gave me a fist bump
and we walked off towards Dad's car. She was
talking to someone pretty important in the art
gallery world by the sounds of the conversation.

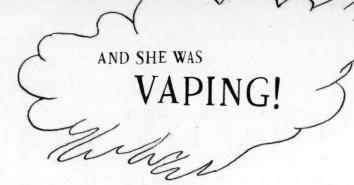

AND SHE WAS
VAPING!

'WHAT THE . . .?' I heard Dad mutter.

'Shut it, Dad . . . or I promise . . . I will actually kill you,' I growled.

But, flipping heck, she looked COOL. She looks more like Harmony's age than mine now – ripped jeans, deadly trainers, trendy canvas rucksack chucked over her shoulder and plaits in her long hair, which is much lighter than it used to be. And a DOUBLE-WHOPPER 'with-it' knee-length green coat.

I need to get Mum to take me to London and get some new gear.

Finally Aleeshaa's VIP phone call finished.

'Hell-o, Alee-shaa,' Dad said in some stupid voice that adults use when they want to be noticed.

'Hello, Mr Hopkinson,' Aleeshaa replied, blowing a big cloud out of her vape.

'I'd rather you didn't do that in the car, if it's all the same to you,' Dad said. Parents are so embarrassing.

So I just rolled my eyes at Aleeshaa and ran my fingers across my throat a few times.

'So, check you out, girl,' Aleeshaa said, ignoring Dad as we drove off. 'I LOOOVE those wellington boots . . . Right on it.'

What the flipping heck was she on about? My boots are the same as everyone else's – even Vince and Vinnie's – but I guess when in Rome you've got to walk the walk – so I gave a cool shrug of my shoulders.

'Hey . . . I'm so excited about this gig . . . You're a dark horse, Holly Hopkinson,' she said, giving me another fist bump.

I nodded. 'Well, that's the way we roll around here.'

Dad tried to catch my eye in his mirror while he pulled a moose face – I should have given him a few verses of my MAGIC POCKET WATCH before we set off. But thankfully, for once in his life, Dad put a sock in it.

It would appear, however, that I may have given Aleeshaa the impression that The Cool were playing a gig tonight. So I was going to have to get my ducks lined up with their mouths shut DOUBLE-WHOPPER fast.

Such as (right order) – it rained before the driver Sir Walter Rally put his cloak across a puddle for Queen Elizabeth to step on, to avoiding getting her shoes wet.

Or (wrong order) – some flipping idiot had dug a big hole in the road before it filled up with rainwater and Sir Walter put his cloak over it. So the queen got a right ducking when she stepped on to the cloak.

In those days it was the difference between being given a palace to live in or having your head cut off while one of your legs was taken to Dover at the same time that your other leg was on its way to York – not a nice experience if your legs left first.

Well, that was the situation that Holly Hopkinson – band manager and gig organiser – had to sort out if she wasn't going to look like some DOUBLE-WHOPPER doofus, thank you very much.

It was time to get EXPRESSO with my MAGIC POCKET WATCH, as they say in Wales.

When we got back to the farm, the first thing that Aleeshaa spotted – even before the amount of animal poo she had to hopscotch her way through – was that her phone had no signal.

'I can't believe it . . . No signal,' she moaned.

Which gave me my first big break of the day.

'Follow me, Aleeshaa . . . If you stand on your tiptoes in Harmony's bedroom, you can get some . . . She's away protesting . . . Here we are . . . I'll be back in a minute.'

I raced out to the recording shed where Harold, Stickly and Badger were just hanging out being doofus mooses.

'Gather round,' I commanded.

I gave them four verses of **SPIRO, SPERO** in case they got diluted among three of them – which they did not – the three of them looked like a proper pop group by the time I'd finished – totally GOGGLE-EYED.

'I am about to introduce you to a spy for a London band . . . She is here to steal your songs . . . and she thinks you're playing a gig tonight but you're not . . . It's just been cancelled . . . And you won't play one note in front of her . . . It's for your own good . . .

COMPRENDO?

Everyone nodded.

89

'Events, dear boy, events,' said Harold.

I've worked out that it is *good* for The Cool if no one hears them for a bit – certainly until Badger's settled in and Stickly stops showing off and stuff – so that's why the **MAGIC POCKET WATCH** worked. But 'events' were moving fast. By the time I'd sorted The Cool out, Daffodil had arrived outside the studio.

She and Aleeshaa were sort of sniffing each other like Barkley did when he met the poodle in the park in London. Although their noses weren't in THAT place.

'BON JOURNO, Daffodil,' I said, welcoming my countryside best friend. And then I did a dramatic whirl with my arms in the direction of Aleeshaa. 'So this is the one and only coolest London best friend ever . . . Aleeshaa of the Black Hebesphenomegacorona gallery in Notting Hill.'

But Aleeshaa didn't exactly blossom under the warmth of my words.

'Yeah . . . Daffodil says she's been your best friend since you got moved down here.'

'Excuse you,' I replied. 'It was a voluntary journey . . . We were not transplanted here like a flock of dustbin foxes, thank you very much.'

But I WAS quite pleased that Daffodil had chucked in some best friend stuff. Because officially our friendship status has never actually been called off, even though Daffodil has been riding loose and fast with Felicity Snoop.

'Wot eva . . . Anyway . . . where's the recordin' studio?' Aleeshaa asked.

 'STUDIO?' chimed Daffodil unhelpfully.

91

Now I may have talked quite a big game to Aleeshaa about the recording shed – studio – but that's the way we roll. Anyway, Harold, Stickly and Badger were chewing the breeze and being cool when we got in there – but not a music note in sight.

'So this is Harold, my brother – did you meet in London . . .? Of course you did – and this is Stickly, and that over there is Badger.'

'Hiya . . . I don't think so . . . Nice to meet you too,' Aleeshaa replied, which was a bit of a slap in the face with a wet herring for Harold, who'd been nodding like a cheap plastic toy when I introduced Aleeshaa.

'Nice trainers,' observed Badger. 'Respect.'

'Yeah . . . well, where's the recordin' studio?' Aleeshaa asked, twisting her neck round as if she was looking for a missing bat.

'This is it, man . . . This is where we make our magic,' Harold informed her with a SHEEPISH GRIN on his face.

'Oh . . . yeah . . . I see . . . Random . . . Where's the gig tonight, then?'

There was a bit of a silence until my ex-country best friend (with immediate effect) Daffodil Chichester chirped, 'What gig?'

'Never you mind, Daffodil . . . It's been cancelled at the last minute . . . It got struck by lightning,' I announced officially.

'That sucks . . . Gigs never get cancelled for lightnin' in London,' Aleeshaa informed us.

'Lightning?' chirped Daffodil again.

And just as I was about to ask my former countryside best friend if she had turned into one of those machines that repeat everything you say, guess which unlikely saviour came to my rescue?

'ALL RIIGHT.'

'Vinnie . . . what a lovely surprise . . . This is my friend Aleeshaa.'

'ALL RIIGHT.'

'Vinnie . . . would you like to drive Aleeshaa around the farm on the tractor . . .? She comes from London so she doesn't know stuff . . . Daffodil and I will come too . . . won't we, Daffodil?'

'No thanks . . . My mum says if I come home smelling of sheep's doings again, I can wash my own clothes . . . I'm fine here, thanks.'

So Vinnie and I took Aleeshaa on a guided tour of the farm – not that she seemed that interested because she was doing her text messages most of the time.

Then, just as I was about to suggest some cool things that we could do, she had a bombshell announcement.

'I've got to go back to London . . . My father needs me at the gallery . . . Some very important international clients are arriving . . .'

'But I thought you were staying over, Aleeshaa?' I said, trying to hold it together.

'I know . . . tradge . . . maybe another time . . . Can your pet take me to the station on this thing?'

'Excuse you . . . he is not my pet . . . Vinnie is a very skilled operator, I'll have you know.'

Anyway, me and Vinnie had the last laugh – we dropped her off by the path to the village where there's always steaming horse POO.

With any luck there'll have been fresh supplies and she'll have been up to her waist in it. And ponging like anything all the way back to London.

THE FLIPPING CHEEK

OF IT – CALLING VINNIE MY PET.

You are never going to guess who was VERY put out that Aleeshaa had to go back to London!

YES.

My DOOFUS brother Harold.

'Events, dear boy, events,' he muttered when he heard the bad news and sloped off to his bedroom to squeeze one of his spots.

CHAPTER 10

THE PHOENIX RISES

MUM CAME OUT ALL GUNS BLAZING THIS MORNING. BLIMEY, MY **MAGIC POCKET WATCH** IS STRONG STUFF.

She was like a ballerina in a cheese shop. I think I may have overcooked her.

Anyway, she had a clipboard with her action points on it when she made her entry into the kitchen. And she was speaking in her 'guru' voice.

'GOOD MORNING, LADIES AND GENTLEMEN . . . IF I CAN CALL THE MEETING TO ACTION, I HAVE THREE AREAS TO COVER.'

And didn't she just!

✗ ACTION ONE – She's decided to overhaul the Hopkinson family. We have been turned into a spreadsheet.

Harold's been told to prepare a SWOT analysis of himself. I thought a swot was someone like Felicity Snoop who sucks up to teachers, but it turns out 'SWOT' means 'Strengths-Weaknesses-Opportunities-Threats'.

✗ ACTION TWO – Harmony's got to do a five at five every day. Which means she's got to tell Mum what she's up to for five minutes every time it's five o'clock – except in the morning – luckily for her Mum's asleep then.

✗ ACTION THREE – Mum has decided to maximise the opportunities in the farmyard. The Cool's recording shed has made her think other businesses could also move in.

PROTESTING NEWS – you WILL NOT believe what else Mum's going to do.

- YES. -

She's going to join Harmony demonstrating outside Union Jack Porker's Happy Farm. So I think we can take it that her career as a PR guru might be over. Finished.

Nuked.

Exterminated.

Anyway, before I got rebranded by Mum, I decided to scarper.

So I donned my racing manager hat and went with Grandpa to see Le Prince, and Declan of course.

Vinnie was riding Le Prince around the field, so 'the lady who brushes', Grandpa and I chewed some grass, leaned on the gate and watched them. They were looking good.

'No sign of Vince this morning,' I observed to 'the lady who brushes'. But she was too busy fussing around Grandpa making sure he wasn't catching a chill.

'I said there's no sign of Vince this morning,' I repeated in my 'outdoor' voice.

There is <u>NOTHING</u> worse than adults who don't listen.

'He's sorting out his houses planning application,' she finally muttered.

'Good,' I replied. 'Stickly and his family won't have to sleep rough after all.'

(It was only later that I realised that she had muttered 'HOUSES' and not 'house'.)

When Vinnie had finished doing his stuff with Le Prince, I pulled him to one side and told him that our priorities had changed.

'The thing is,' I told Vinnie out of the corner of my mouth, 'there are no short-term targets for Le Prince . . . We can take our time with him . . . but Declan, well, he's a different matter.'

'All riight,' Vinnie replied with a confused and pained expression on his face.

I had to spell it out.

'GET DECLAN OUT OF THE GARAGE AND START TEACHING HIM STUFF . . . COMPRENDO?'

Sometimes Vinnie understands better if you talk to him quite loudly – and partly in a different language. It's just one of his quirks.

'We've got to get Declan ready for the Chequers Xmas Pony Race . . . and you've got to teach me to ride him . . . so that I can stick it to the rest of our class.'

Vinnie nodded. 'All riight.'

Grandpa and I dropped in on Dad and Aunt Electra AGAIN at the Chequers on our way home to offer a bit of customer feedback. (The soup smelled like Harold's socks.)

It was also an opportunity for me to remind Aunt Electra that:

1. She hasn't **OFFICIALLY** got any dates on the Chequers Xmas Entertainments Calendar when The Cool will be playing.

2. The Cool are getting booked up fast and have been invited to go on a virtual-reality TV talent show. (That is not strictly true, but in the music business you have to wing the smoke-and-mirrors-dazzling-people bit if you want to get on.)

Then the dotty woman asked me if The Cool can sing Christmas carols.

'Carols?' I replied. 'Excuse you.' You just couldn't make it up.

If she doesn't spit-spot pull her finger out, the Chequers is going to miss out one hundred per cent on The Cool and whose fault is that going to be?

Dad was experimenting with curry powder in the kitchen. His butcher friend Sir Garfield has brought round a bag of animal spare parts for Dad to practise with.

Dad's working on a special **EXOTIC** 'meal deal' menu for the over-eighties. Everything is going through the machine that turns the whole lot into liquid, so it doesn't matter if they haven't got any teeth.

He says the TV cook Heston Bloomingdale does stuff like this and you have to wear headphones like Harold's to get the full effect. But I'm not sure that I want to hear cows mooing in a field while I eat their liquidised cousins, thank you very much.

FIRST COURSE – all the leftover vegetables and some curry powder (liquidised)

 MAIN COURSE – Sir Garfield's animal parts and some curry powder (liquidised)

 PUDDING – one of Vera's cakes, some curry powder and fizzy orange (liquidised)

☆ **CHEESE AND BISCUITS** – (liquidised).

Anyway, the **IDYLLIC** peace and quiet of a genteel country bistro pub then got blown to smithereens. Mrs Smartside arrived and, boy, she was kicking off.

'What is the meaning of THIS?' she bellowed at Aunt Electra, waving a copy of the Chequers Christmas Entertainments Calendar in the air. 'You have stolen the Village Cultural Events Organising Committee's entire Christmas programme.'

Aunt Electra just looked very **BOHEMIAN**, like she can do, and called Mrs Smartside a 'ridiculous woman'. She should get a bravery medal when the politicians next hand them out to all their mates.

But panic has broken out in the world of Holly Hopkinson. My life is in danger of going down the pain au chocolate, if you'll pardon my French.

What if Mrs Smartside starts torturing Aunt Electra to find out who her source was? I will be toast because I don't think they can cope with much pain in Bohemia.

And then Mrs Smartside will sell me to a workhouse to make Mrs Chichester's embroidered candles and smelly cushions before I'm burned at the stake.

'You shall be hearing from my lawyers,' was Mrs Smartside's final cry as she stormed out of the pub like a galleon in full sail with a **HURRICANE** up its backside.

THAT WAS A
DOUBLE-WHOPPER
NEAR MISS.

PROTESTING NEWS – Mum looked a bit odd when she and Harmony got back from Happy Farm.

'So how did it go, ladies?' Dad asked.

'It was, like, sooo cool . . . There were TV cameras there . . . and, like, really cool people chanting . . . and Mum got interviewed by the news people.'

'Oh . . . Mum got interviewed, did she . . ? Well, that will be good for her future employment prospects, won't it?' Dad replied. He looked excessively impertinent, like Moggy.

'Well . . . I don't suppose anyone will see it,' Mum said defensively.

But before Dad could pull any more **idiotic** faces, Mum used her PR 'nuclear-deterrent' skills and sent a missile in Grandpa's direction.

'Grandpa, what is Vince up to?' she asked as she brandished a bit of yellow paper in the air. 'I found THIS pinned up outside the railway station.'

'No idea,' replied Grandpa from behind his newspaper.

'Is Vince kidding?' Mum now asked Dad in a new 'outdoor protesting' voice that she's developed. 'A hundred new houses on the edge of Lower Goring? Really?'

I gulped and did my frog-swallowing-a-fly impersonation.

'ER . . . WHAT'S HAPPENING, MUM?'

I asked.

'Vince has put in an application to build a hundred houses on the edge of the village next to Mrs Smartside's orchard . . . Can you believe it?'

Dad starting laughing. 'He's brave.'

'It's not funny, George,' Mum said. 'We DO NOT want the village spoiled by one hundred new houses.'

'I wonder what's made him do that?' I asked.

'Well . . . it might be a good thing,' suggested Dad. 'More people to eat in the pub.'

'But **HORRENDOUS** people from the towns will come and live in them,' Mum protested.

'Only this morning you were talking about developing Grandpa's sheds,' Dad reminded Mum.

'Well, that's different,' Mum said, and NO ONE was going to disagree with her.

'We're, like, sooo going to protest,' announced Harmony. 'Will you come and climb trees with us, Holly?'

'Er . . . I'm a bit scared of heights, actually.'

What the flipping heck is Vince thinking? My **MAGIC POCKET WATCH** and I told him to build ONE house for Stickly and his family, not ONE HUNDRED.

CHAPTER 11
INTERNATIONAL TV NEWS

SO MUCH FOR MUM THINKING NO ONE
WAS GOING TO SEE HER INTERVIEWED
OUTSIDE **HAPPY FARM**.

'It's you, Sally,' Grandpa shouted. 'You're on the TV.'

'Whaat?' said Mum.

And, sure enough, there was Mum in full flow on TV.

'THESE PIES ARE NOT ENGLISH ... THEY COME FROM SOMEWHERE YOU WOULD NOT WANT TO GO TO ... THEY ARE POISONOUS ... THEY ARE NOT HAPPY ... THIS FACTORY SHOULD BE SHUT DOWN.'

And then the police stepped in and started hassling Mum.

'Well, no one's going to see that, are they?' Dad chirped up.

'Mum . . . you look a bit mad . . . Look at your eyes . . . and your hair . . . and your TEETH,' I said.

'Well, the wind was blowing,' Mum said SHEEPISHLY.

So Holly Hopkinson's mother is now an UNEMPLOYABLE GURU, and at this rate her father won't be far behind!

CHAPTER 12

MRS SMARTSIDE'S UNDIES

SO I WAITED TILL THE DUST HAD SETTLED
AND THE ADULTS HAD ALL BRUSHED THEIR
TEETH AND PUT THEMSELVES DOWN. THEN I
SNEAKED UP TO HARMONY'S ROOM TO GIVE
HER THE **LOWDOWN NEWS.**

'You can't go and protest about the houses Vince
wants to build,' I told Harmony. 'Because he's
going to build a house for Stickly and his family –
otherwise they'll be sleeping rough.'

'Well, why is he, like, sooo trying to build
a hundred houses?' Harmony wanted to know.

'Probably because he isn't very good at counting
. . . Look at Vinnie . . . He hasn't exactly been
snapped up by Mensa yet, has he?'

'But I told Mum I'd, like, go and chain myself to a tree tomorrow.'

'Well, tell her you've lost the key and got **OFFICIAL** song-writing practice with The Cool tomorrow . . . and I'll see if I can rearrange the numbers in Vince's head.'

Harmony didn't look convinced, so I dripped a few lines in about Stickly having to sleep under cardboard and she agreed to go along with it.

Anyway, guess who pitched up the next morning at the farm, looking like she'd never spilled any milk on her new breeches?

YES.

Daffodil Chichester and her mother. Daffodil has not found out that Aleeshaa went back to London early. So I can still big up my friendship with Aleeshaa to her.

But it turned out her journey to our farmyard wasn't a bid by Daffodil to get herself reconfirmed as my **OFFICIAL** countryside best friend.

No. It turns out that Mum is going to rent Mrs Chichester a 'retail outlet' – otherwise known as a hay shed.

Of course, Aunt Electra's carry-on at the village fete is what has inspired this U-bend development – who ever heard of selling embroidered candles and cushions smelling of scent in a desserted* farmyard next to a recording shed?

While Mum and Mrs Chichester were making their shopping mall plans I took Daffodil up to my bedroom to clear up what exactly our best friend status is at the moment. But, as I was about to break the ice, she said, 'Holly . . . I think you should know that Felicity Snoop and I are **BEST FRIENDS** again now that we're riding together every day.'

* DESSERTED – empty place not to be confused with puddings.

Talk about getting a slap in the face with a wet turbot – I had NOT seen that one coming.

This is **DEATH** by a thousand cuts, including my head, stomach and most of my limbs. Next it will be my body parts being scattered all over Chipping Topley and the surrounding area.

'Well, of course that means you will have to give up your membership of the Bogey Club,' I said sharply.

'Oh,' said Daffodil.

HA – she hadn't thought that one through.

As if my day wasn't going badly enough, guess who then came tearing down the drive as if she's a sheriff?

YES.

Mrs Smartside. That was all I needed, thank you very much.

I could not let her catch me – AT ANY COST – which made Daffodil a security risk.

So I gave her my marching orders and told her 'it' is over between us OFFICIALLY. Then I took up my snooping position in the haystack on my own, TOOT SUITE.

'LADIES . . . I AM IN DISTRESS,'

wailed Mrs Smartside as she threw herself into Mum and Mrs Chichester's arms. (Well, that is a bit of exaggeration but there was some body contact.)

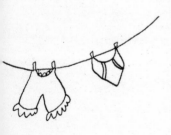

It turned out that Vince's planning application for the houses has thrown her into a spin. Apparently everyone living in the new houses will be able to see Mrs Smartside's underwear on the washing line (that should stop the buyers' stampede).

'Charmian . . . Sally . . . you will both have to be joint chairwomen of the Anti-Housing and Development of the Village Campaign,' Mrs Smartside demanded. 'I will have to take a back seat and refrain from giving my excellent opinion so that people can't say I have a selfish interest. Oh, my view . . . It will be ruined.'

'Um . . . when you say "development" . . . would that affect farmyards?' Mum asked.

'Oh . . . don't worry about farmyards . . . Who cares about them . . . ? It's MY beautiful view, Sally, that's about to be turned into a housing estate.'

'Oh good . . . just checking . . . That's OK, then.'

'And another thing, Sally . . . The Chequers has stolen our Christmas events programme this year. And YOU need to find out WHO leaked the information or heads will have to roll.'

It was time to slip off to the Bogey Club for a bit of peace and quiet. As I skulked out of the farmyard I could hear Mum shouting, 'Holly . . . Holly . . . where are you . . . ? I need to speak to you

RIGHT NOW!'

117

Vinnie has taught me how to wolf whistle – and I can now make a terrific noise that scares the living daylights out of Barkley – and Vera.

Basically you stick your fingers in your mouth and then blow air through them and the racket is unbelievable.

After we'd done a load of practice I crept up behind Vera in the kitchen while she was knocking up one of her chemical warfare dishes and gave her a good blast.

The result was DOUBLE-WHOPPER hilarious – she went absolutely berserk and her toxic concoction sprayed everywhere.

Grandpa thought it was hilarious but HE had to make a big deal of telling me off in front of the shaking Vera.

CHAPTER 13

FRIENDLESS

GRANDPA AND I SET OFF TO SEE DECLAN
AND LE PRINCE BEFORE BREAKFAST. I WAS
THINKING OF GIVING VINNIE THE NEWS
THAT HE COULD NOW **OFFICIALLY** BE MY
BEST FRIEND.

Le Prince was in his stable with Billy the sheep, which suited Grandpa – he could just watch 'the lady who brushes' brushing him. Meanwhile Vinnie was putting Declan through his paces out in the field. Declan looked pretty nifty for a horse that has apparently been shrunk by his last owner.

'Vinnie, I wouldn't want to give you the impression that I already know what sort of race we will be running in at the Chequers Xmas Pony Race, but I could have a few guesses that might be right,' I said in my 'inside knowledge' voice.

'All riight,' Vinnie said.

'So I think we can assume there will be a dash from the front of the Chequers round the church, past the ruined hall and back to the Chequers – so you need to get Declan happy running in a left-hand circle.'

'All riight.'

'And then we'll have to go flat out in a straight line before slamming the brakes on.'

'All riight.'

'Then there just might be a sort of bending race, so he'll have to be pretty spit-spot diving to the left and right.'

'All riight.'

'And, one other thing, make sure Declan doesn't mind the smell of cow poo – because Aunt Electra might have a farmyard version of apple bobbing on her mind.'

'All riight.'

'And then, when Declan's learned that lot, you'd better teach me how to ride him . . .'

Then Vinnie had quite a good idea. In words of no syllables he suggested that I should launch my riding career on Beanstalk; if Beanstalk was amenable to such a plan. He would have a word with her later.

My feet might need roller-skates, but at least I won't have far to fall.

So that is Plan A.

As we leaned over the gate chewing grass, guess who came along?

YES.

Trainer Vince in his new trainer's outfit.

'So you've put in for planning permission for a lot of houses,' I said to Vince, giving him a look.

'Ah,' he replied. (You have to remember he is Vinnie's uncle.)

'I thought you were just going to build one house for Stickly's family?' I pointed out.

At this point Vince struggled to get all his words out in the right order. Suffice to say that Vince thought if it was a good idea to build one house, it was **a hundred** times better idea to build a hundred houses.

'Well, you'll have demonstrations,' I pointed out. 'So you might want some advice from me how to deal with that. I DO have some influence around the village, you know.'

'Ah.'

So I think Vince is now one of my PR clients, which will be handy when it comes to buying my iPad. But what I really need to do here is be like the Swiss and get some loot from both camps.

Then I remembered that I hadn't given Vinnie the good news.

'Vinnie,' I said, giving him my cute smile, 'I nearly forgot to tell you that you are now OFFICIALLY my best friend,' I said.

Vinnie did not exactly throw himself into my arms – in fact, he looked distinctly shifty. 'Er, can't be.'

'WHAT?'

'Can't be – Prince's me best friend,' he spluttered, getting more than one word in the right order, albeit at the wrong time, thank you very much.

'But Le Prince is a horse.'

'RIIGHT.'

'Well, horses can't hang out with you and shoot the breeze.'

'Prince can, all riight,' Vinnie replied like a moose.

This is the sort of stuff you have to deal with if you move out of London to a farmyard with derelict people.

How CAN it be possible that I have a **MAGIC POCKET WATCH** and NO official best friend?

THIS IS NOT A GOOD STATE OF AFFAIRS IN THE MEMOIRS OF HOLLY HOPKINSON.

SHOPPING NEWS – Grandpa and I popped into Chipping Topley on the way home. Grandpa was being dead shifty about what he was up to but I had a pretty good idea what was going on.

Why else would he want to go to the ladies' gift section in the charity shop? Obviously to buy 'the lady who brushes' more brushes.

Grandpa is making a move on her – but if Vera finds out he'll be found at the bottom of the river with a couple of her cakes tied round his ankles.

He may want to pay me a PR fee to keep this quiet – like half an iPad's worth?

CHAPTER 14

BEANSTALK TO THE RESCUE

SO VINNIE SAYS HE'S HAD A CHAT WITH
BEANSTALK, AND SHE IS HAPPY TO
HELP OUT TEACHING ME TO RIDE.

Beanstalk is titchy but still quite scary – even
when I have roller-skates on.

'You have told her no funny business, haven't
you Vinnie?' I checked. 'You know what they say
about small ponies? They bite at one end and kick
at the other.'

'She's all riight,' was Vinnie's response.

What I had not expected was an audience. First
Grandpa shows up, then Harold, Harmony, Stickly
and Badger suspended band practice – which they
can ill afford to do – to come and watch.

'The Earwigs, or whoever they were, didn't write "Stairway to Heaven" mooning about in a farmyard watching rodeos,' I pointed out.

Then Vera of all people raised her **MISERABLE** head from washing Grandpa's undies to come and have a snoop, even though she doesn't approve of horses.

Even Mum broke off her Anti-Housing and Development of the Village Campaign meeting, which she was having with herself, and came to watch too. So I told her to make herself useful and tighten the straps on my roller-skates.

Although Beanstalk is quite small, she is a bit excitable and springy – and her hair is rather thick and matted and could do with a session with 'the lady who brushes'.

Vinnie led me round the field and Beanstalk just walked, thank goodness. I wasn't up for galloping or jumping or stuff like that on my first day. But the OFFICIAL riding career of Holly Hopkinson has been launched without any undesirable events.

MAIN NEWS today —

Mum has called a family meeting that everyone has to attend – even Vera and Vinnie have been told it's turn up or else. And Dad was told he had to cancel going to London to do some celebrity chef-ing – he was due at the launch of what Mum called 'not another cookbook'.

MY DAD HAS TURNED INTO ONE
OF THOSE IDIOT CELEBRITIES
THAT WILL WALK MILES AS LONG AS
THERE'S A RED CARPET UNDERFOOT
AND CAMERAS CLICKING – AND
FREE SANDWICHES.

Back to Mum's meeting – 'Quiet, everyone,' she said in her 'Mrs Smartside' voice. 'The Hopkinson family must decide where we stand on Vince's house-building application to the council . . . That includes you too, Vera and Vinnie.'

'I shall propose that we all stand shoulder to shoulder against it,' declared Mum, casting her beady eye around the room. Are we all agreed?' she asked RHEUMATOIDICALLY.

This was a good moment for Holly Hopkinson to put a sock in it and let someone else, like my sister, take the firing squad.

'That's, like, sooo not right . . . I think Vince should build houses for people who don't have anywhere to live.'

'Oh, really . . . I thought you were going to be climbing trees to protest, young lady,' snorted Mum.

'Well, I, like, sooo changed my mind,' said Harmony.

'Good for you,' said Dad. 'Very open-minded of you, Harmony.'

'Hardly, George,' said Mum huffily. 'All you're thinking of are new customers.'

'Pubs need chimneypots around them, my dear,' Dad replied. He only calls her 'my dear' when he's winding her up. It doesn't mean he thinks she's being 'dear'.

'HAROLD?' Mum barked. 'Well . . .¿'

'Events, dear boy, events. The working-class folk have got to have somewhere to live, man.'

Mum did an eyebrow swivel and made a noise a little bit like Declan does when he's having a poo in his stable – different result luckily.

Dad had a mischievous chuckle with himself.

'Grandpa, surely YOU can't be in favour of seeing Vince's green and pleasant fields get concreted over?' Mum asked.

Grandpa just happened to have a coughing fit at that very moment. But Mum wasn't going to be fobbed off by a **life-threatening** blockage. She just waited for it to clear.

'Well, Vince has been a friend for a long time . . . and farming is tough these days,' Grandpa pointed out.

'But, Sally,' interrupted Aunt Electra, 'aren't you about to do some developing yourself . . . starting with a retail outlet for Mrs Chichester?'

Mum went red like she'd just done some bottom music and said the two things were NOT connected.

Nobody bothered to ask Vinnie what he thought and Vera had just disappeared into thin air.

And just when I thought I'd managed to duck the issue Mum spotted me trying not to be spotted. 'Holly . . . pray share your thoughts with us,' Mum demanded in a very un-prayer like manner.

'Well, I was thinking I could be neutral and see how things go,' I suggested. 'Then I can help all of you.'

You see, I'm thinking Swiss here. My family could give me all their stuff and then have a good scrap with each other.

GOOD PLAN.

Mum sniffed. 'I'm sure you will, young lady.'

SO IT'S OFFICIAL –
THE HOPKINSON FAMILY ARE SPLIT –
ALTHOUGH MOST OF THEM ARE AGAINST MUM.
BUT I NEED TO MAKE SURE I'M
PLAYING BOTH SETS OF CARDS.

CHAPTER 15

VINCE'S YULETIDE LOG COMPETITION

SO THE FIRST MAJOR VILLAGE
EVENT OF THE XMAS SEASON TO BE HELD
SINCE THE UNVEILING OF THE CHEQUERS
RIVAL XMAS ENTERTAINMENT SCHEDULE
AND VINCE'S NUCLEAR HOUSING
APPLICATION BOMBSHELL WAS HIS
YULETIDE LOG COMPETITION.

Vince had no idea that he was walking into a potential water cannon situation when he arrived at the village hall with his Yuletide log tucked under his armpit, like it was a duck.

On one side of the hall Mum and Mrs Chichester and few of their gang were making childish hissing noises like you've never heard. If we did that at school, we'd be in the flipping corridor for the rest of the day. And none of them had brought a log with them, so they could hardly complain when they didn't win.

On the other side Aunt Electra (she's got some neck showing up in the village hall after her antics) and Stickly were agitating and generally stirring the cud. They had a whole stack of logs decorated on the tables in front of them, although a few of them still had their Made in China stickers on them, so that's cheating.

Vinnie got egged on by Stickly and started doing stuff with his fingers that you shouldn't do in public.

\ | | / /
~ **_SURPRISE NEWS (NOT)_** – Daffodil was a NO-SHOW – probably brushing her NEW pony with Felicity Snoop in matching outfits.

Mrs Smartside was sitting on the stage with the vicar next to her, but half her size, twitching like he was one of her dogs.

'The vicar will speak,' she announced in her 'deep' voice. 'Some decorum please.'

Reluctantly both sides stopped making farmyard noises at each other.

'ER ... GOOD EVENING ... AGH ... NICE TO SEE YOU ALL ... HMPF ... COMPLIMENTS OF THE FESTIVE SEASON,'

he stuttered, throwing in a nervous giggle.

'UM ... THE YULETIDE LOG COMPETITION ... YERPS ... WELL, IT SEEMS WE MAY HAVE TO DELAY THINGS GIVEN THE LOCAL DIFFERENCES.'

'Judas,' someone in the crowd shouted in 'Vince's' voice.

The vicar went red like he'd done one.

'We've got our logs here so one of us should be the winner,' shouted another member of the rabble in 'Aunt Electra's' voice.

'Well, the sponsor has withdrawn,' screeched someone from the opposite side of the room in 'Mrs Chichester's' voice.

'I'm sponsor,' Vince pointed out. ''Ave been for years.'

'Well, not this year – a new sponsor was found and ratified at a committee meeting YOU didn't turn up to!' Mrs Chichester said in her 'sponsor's' voice.

'LADIES . . . VINCENT . . . PLEASE REMEMBER WHERE WE ARE,'

the vicar pleaded.

'The village hall,' Vince reminded him. 'What has that got to do with anything? Tonight is the Yuletide Log Competition, and if they don't enter, they can't win. But it doesn't stop us winning.'

And then they all kicked off again and someone who shall remain NAMELESS threw one of the logs at the stage and it took the vicar down.

CHAPTER 16

MUM PULLS IN HER TROOPS

SO GRANDPA, 'THE LADY WHO BRUSHES', VINCE AND I WERE LEANING OVER THE GATE WATCHING VINNIE PUT DECLAN THROUGH HIS PACES. AND EVERYTHING WAS GOING OK UNTIL DECLAN TOOK OFF ACROSS THE FIELD LIKE HIS BACKSIDE WAS ON FIRE.

It took Vinnie some time to calm him down.

'What was that about? I thought you two were mates?' I asked.

'Riight,' said Vinnie, thoroughly exhausted. 'Declan's got very sensitive hearing and something frightened him.'

Then I started to hear the noise too – and it got

louder –
  and louder –
    and louder

until EVEN Grandpa could hear it when the 'lady who brushes' stopped cooing into his ear like a pigeon for one second.

'Wat's tha'?' asked Vince.

'It sounds like a lot of people, that's what tha' is,' I said. 'Come on, let's go and see.'

And guess who'd appeared outside the gates of Vince's farmyard?

- YES. -

Mum and her merry band of men and women, who are NOW the Anti-Housing and Development of the Village Campaign.

Mum isn't a retired PR guru for nothing. She has persuaded everyone who gets the train from Chipping Topley to London that if Vince builds a hundred houses there won't be any seats on the train FOR THEM.

And Mrs Chichester has told all her customers that if Vince is allowed to build a **hundred houses**, their builders, and even gardeners, will be able to live in the same village as them. Well, that sent electric shocks through the ladies that lunch. So loads of HER people turned up too.

— BIG NEWS —

Vera has joined up with Mum and Mrs Chichester. So much for blood being stickier than water; you'd have thought she'd be on her nephew Vince's side.

— GOSSIP NEWS — Some idiot (Vinnie, I'm 110 per cent sure) has sneaked on Grandpa about the amount of time he's been spending with 'the lady who brushes'. And the same doofus has also (rightly) given Vera the impression that 'the lady who brushes' is angling for Grandpa to buy her one of these new houses.

Holly Hopkinson reporting from the front line – THIS IS A HOPKINSON FAMILY FARRAGO.

LATE NEWS – no sign of Harmony; she's ALSO trying to play a Swiss card, it would appear.

CHAPTER 17

LOWER GORING XMAS PONY SHOW

I NEVER THOUGHT I'D SEE THE DAY WHEN I'D BE SKULKING LIKE A RUNAWAY PRISONER IN A DITCH IN THE MIDDLE OF NOWHERE.

Vinnie was also with me, but do not assume the two of us spying on the village Christmas pony show involves any Bonnie and Clyde type BOGGLE-EYED carry-on, THANK you very much. We were strictly doing reconnaissance* stuff so I can take down the rest of my class at the Chequers Xmas Pony Race. Which will have better prizes and more food.

Our ditch, half full of water, was the perfect place to watch and earwig on the mothers of the Lower Goring Pony Club sprogs.

* RECONNAISSANCE –
a new way of spying.

140

TWO THINGS TO NOTE:

1. **THE MOTHERS** can be divided into three categories:

A) **MRS CHICHESTER TYPES** – all the gear and no idea. She had some ridiculous blue flowery dress on like you see in magazines in places you don't want to be – like the dentist. With my red-herring hearing, I heard Mrs Chichester talk about 'having to give away prizes'.

B) **VERA TYPES** – the bossy know-it-alls. Everyone is frightened of them – even the ponies – and their bite is a lot worse than their bark.

C) **MRS SNOOP TYPES (FELICITY'S MOTHER)** – these are super-professional nuts, and they know their onions when they're in Majorca. They've been at it for so long their faces and their bottoms look VERY like their ponies'.

2. **THE KIDS** – I have **OFFICIALLY** put them into three groups:

A) **THE DAFFODILS OF THIS WORLD** – who have just got it all a bit WRONG. Pink jodhpurs? Ple-eease. And her pony looks like it's been to the car wash in Chipping Topley this morning. It's as white as the driven snow before the dogs cocked their legs.

B) **THE KIDS THAT LOOK LIKE VINNIE'S COUSINS** – with most of their breakfast still on their faces.

C) **IRIS, CROCUS, AMARYLLIS AND FELICITY SNOOP TYPES** – **MISS PERFECTS**. Trotting around in their Pony Club ties, plaited pigtails and clothes that fit. And

THEY THINK THEY
KNOW IT ALL.

Felicity Snoop looks like she owns the place – which, as Vinnie pointed out, she does.

The first event that we spied on was the bending race.

WHAT A WASHOUT THAT WAS.

All they had to do was pick up a cup off one pole, meander down through a few cones and stick it on another pole – then make a big fuss about high-fiving the rest of their team – at the walk.

The boys beat the girls because Crocus's pony decided it was hungry and stopped to eat something. Her mother (Category C) shouted, 'KICK HIM, **KICK HIM!'**

AND **NO ONE** DID ANYTHING?

They didn't even call the police. So you can add 'savage' to my description of Category-C mothers.

Everyone who was wearing a Pony Club tie got a blue rosette, the winners got a red rosette and the losers got a pink rosette. So the double-whopper DOOFUS MUPPETS all thought they were heroes.

Then they went back to their eager mothers for doughnuts before the next class. Which really got Vinnie's stomach gurgling. I thought he was about to give birth to a flipping alien.

'Excuse you,' I said to Vinnie. 'Pardon your French.'

Next was the Christmas dressing-up competition, sponsored by Chichester Interior Design. And who do you think they all came dressed as?

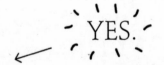

Santa Claus.

And who do you think their ponies came dressed as?

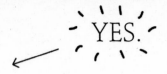

- YES. -

Rudolph.

'You couldn't make this up,' I hissed to Vinnie.

The winners (everyone wearing red with a white beard with a pony that had fake antlers on it) all won a Chichester Interior Design scented cushion, which we couldn't smell from the ditch.

I said, 'Come on, Vinnie, it's time that I had a ride on Declan . . . Let's spit-spot . . . or I am never going to be ready for the Chequers Xmas Pony Race.'

CHAPTER 18

FIRST FALL OFF DECLAN

TROTTING ON A PONY IS A BORE, BECAUSE YOU HAVE TO GO UP-DOWN-UP-DOWN THE **WHOLE TIME**, AND IF YOU'VE JUST HAD A BOWL OF **PORRIDGE** OR ANYTHING COOKED BY VERA, IT FEELS LIKE IT'S GOING TO MAKE A REAPPEARANCE THROUGH A **CHOICE OF EXITS**.

But I think cantering will be a doddle. All you have to do is sit on your bum and squeeze with your legs. What could possibly go wrong?

Well, the first circuit round the field was majestic. I felt like a swan gracefully gliding along on Declan. I was fully expecting Vinnie to want to take up my **irresistible** offer of **BEST FRIEND** status once he'd seen me float by.

146

My legs started to get DOUBLE-WHOPPER tired on the second circuit. Then I totally lost my ability to 'squeeze'. I couldn't have cracked an egg with the amount of 'squeeze' left in my trousers. Although that would have made a right jolly mess if I had done.

So I started bouncing around like a flipping lottery ball in one of those machines that spits the balls out randomly. All I needed was a number on my back.

Then my bum began to hurt on the third circuit – A LOT. In fact, sitting on THE LOO is not going to be an option for a few days.

So, as I was saying 'WOE' really quite loudly to get Declan to stop, a pesky pigeon flapped out of a tree and startled him. He jinked to the left and I went straight on. The first thing that hit the ground was my head.

The second thing was my pride. I felt like a right wally.

I am **never** going to be ready for this flipping pony race – what am I thinking?

'All riight?' Vinnie asked as he and Declan stood over me.

'Well, I've felt better,' I said, putting a brave face on the fact that I had half the solar system buzzing around in front of my eyes.

* ALF RESCO –
an Italian bloke who invented outside toilets.

148

'Declan says 'e's sorry. 'E got startled by a pigeon.'

'Didn't we all?' I replied.

The thing is, riding is a bit harder work than it looks, but I AM NOT going to admit that to Vinnie.

'Riight,' said Vinnie. 'Let's 'ave another go.'

And there was me thinking Vinnie was going to carry me spit-spot back to the sofa for some biscuits and hot choc.

My bum now looks like two raw steaks being marinated overnight and the way I'm walking you'd think I was auditioning for a cowboy film. I've even had to put the loo paper in the fridge.

CHAPTER 19

SECOND RIDE ON DECLAN (ABANDONED)

I WAS WALKING AROUND THIS MORNING AS IF I HAD A BEACH BALL BETWEEN MY KNEES. SO I THOUGHT IT MIGHT BE TIME FOR A DAY OFF RIDING.

But Vinnie is pretty one-tracked-minded.

'Ow about rise up on Declan again?' Vinnie asked, not looking me in the eye.

'Has he got over his fear of pigeons yet?' I asked.

'Well, Declan's Declan.'

'No kidding . . . Well, thank you for that priceless piece of information, Vinnie,' I replied. 'And what's that supposed to mean in plain English, if you don't mind?'

'All riight . . . Well, 'e's still a bit jumpy . . . and upset because Chicken's gone missing . . . but I think 'e'll be all riight.'

It turns out that Declan is not feeling spit-spot right now. And not even up for a trot. According to Vinnie, he hasn't slept as the lunatics from the anti-housing protest have kept him up all night.

So the reunion of Declan and Holly Hopkinson has had to be delayed, which does not bode well for the prospect of us pulling off a victory for the underdog at the Chequers Xmas Pony Race.

CHAPTER 20

THE BATTLE OF LOWER GORING IS ABOUT TO COMMENCE

SO THIS MORNING GRANDPA AND I HAD TO RUN THE GAUNTLET OF THE ANTI-HOUSING AND DEVELOPMENT OF THE VILLAGE CAMPAIGN CAMP TO GET IN TO SEE DECLAN AND LE PRINCE. AND I CAN TELL YOU THAT MY MOTHER AND VERA ARE NOW HANGING OUT WITH SOME **VERY UNDESIRABLE,** PONGING PEOPLE WHO HAVE TURNED UP FROM SOMEWHERE WHERE **THE ROMANS** DIDN'T BUILD ANY BATHS.

By the way, Declan has COMPLETELY gone to pieces – he is suffering from **SLEEP DEPRIVATION** and he says (to Vinnie) that he's developing agro-phobia*. And Chicken is still on the missing list.

* AGRO-PHOBIA – fear of demonstrations in an open space.

As if there wasn't enough noise, another racket came marching down the road today – and guess who was at the front of this lot?

YES.

Aunt Electra!

She has formed the Anti-Anti-Housing and Development of the Village Campaign. They're going to set up camp over the road from the Anti-Housing and Development of the Village Campaign.

Hot on Aunt Electra's heels were Harold, HARMONY, Stickly and Badger.

So Harmony has declared her hand – she is no longer Swiss.

Harold has dug up a few freaks from some swamp. They are building a tree village so they can show off to the TV people. And, of course, the coppers can't get at them if they're up a tree, because they'll do nature wees all over them.

And to add to the general threat to peace and tranquillity Vera has brought along a few offensive weapons she's baked. If they start chucking that lot, the police WILL have to use their water cannons.

Harmony is making banners that say LOCAL HOUSING FOR LOCAL BANDS. She's trying to get Stickly and Badger to help her, but they're just mooning about.

This escalation threatens to tear apart the Hopkinson family. I and my **MAGIC POCKET WATCH** NEED to do something.

When we moved to Lower Goring, we did not expect our peace and quiet to be destroyed by protesters from London. Stuff like that is MEANT to happen in urban areas where it belongs.

CHAPTER 21

THE DUCK RACE CATASTROPHE

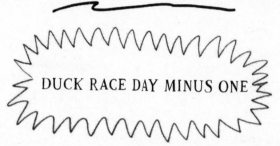

DUCK RACE DAY MINUS ONE

How anything ever gets done in Bohemia I will never know – because Aunt Electra has a habit of being able to start a fight in an empty room.

So when 'the ghastly Mrs Chichester' (Dad's words, not mine) announced the date for the VCEOC Xmas duck race, Aunt Electra OFFICIALLY declared that the Chequers Xmas Duck Race would be on the same day.

That's provunciation* for you, if ever you've heard it.

> * PROVUNCIATION
> – clearly expressed
> confrontation.

But Aunt Electra was so busy winding Mum and the rest of the VCEOC up that she failed to check the one thing that is QUITE IMPORTANT if you're organising a duck race.

IS THERE ANY WATER IN THE RIVER WHERE YOU'RE HAVING THE RACE?

Answer, in Aunt Electra's case – NO.

There is loads of water where the VCEOC are having their race – but then it disappears off down a storm drain by the church bridge.

It was time for Holly Hopkinson to come to the rescue.

There was only one person I could think of to sort this mess out.

YES, VINNIE, OF COURSE.

But by putting my tryst* in Vinnie I'm going to have to put all my eggs into a very loose cannon that is highly likely to break the flipping lot.

* **TRYST** – secret confidence.

156

Grandpa and I went up to Vince's farm to see Le Prince and Declan (still minus Chicken). Which was the perfect moment for me to 'cook' Vinnie.

'Excuse you, Vinnie . . . Could I have a word in the haystack, please?' I asked.

'All riight,' Vinnie said, looking nervous. His animal cunning was telling him they weren't about to fill Declan's hay net.

'Look at my lovely watch, Vinnie . . . Can you see it going backwards and forwards . . . forwards and backwards?' I asked him.

'Aye,' said Vinnie.

'SPIRO, SPERO, SQUIGGLEOUS SCOTCH, CAST YOUR EYES WHITHER MY WATCH.'

I said to Vinnie twice.

I've learned from experience with Vinnie that if I overcook him he goes completely Tonto. So two verses is plenty. The front door of his head doesn't take much opening, if you get my drift.

'Vinnie, I need you to sort the River Topley out for me,' I commanded.

'All riight.'

'It needs to have more water in it from the church bridge past the ruined, haunted hall and down to the Chequers by tomorrow . . . Can you do that?'

'Well, the trouble is—'

'Vinnie . . . Excuse you, but it's a yay or nay, COMPRENDO?'

'Yay,' Vinnie finally said.

So that's another problem solved that no one will probably thank me for, but I'm an outrider.

CHAPTER 22

BREAKING BAND NEWS

THIS IS MY POSITION AS BAND MANAGER AND CAN BE TAKEN AS THE **OFFICIAL** LINE IF ANY PRESS OR MEDIA SHOW UP. ALTHOUGH STICKLY AND HARMONY WERE NEVER 'A HAND-HOLDING ITEM', IF YOU KNOW WHAT I MEAN, THEY WERE **GOOD FRIENDS** ON A PERSONAL AND PROFESSIONAL BASIS.

But it would appear that Stickly has now caught BOGGLE EYES off Badger while they were up a protesting tree, and this HAS NOT gone down well at Chateau Harmony, as they say in Bulgaria.

Because I have to report that Harmony has COME DOWN HER TREE AND crossed the road. She has officially joined Mum in the Anti-Housing and Development of the Village Campaign camp.

Maybe Badger is an infiltration job? The police do things like this to get information on protesters. Sometimes they even marry the people they want to get info off, but I don't think things have gone that far yet.

But Badger is now on my CAVE* list, thank you VERY much.

Just because Harmony has done a switcheroo, you would be wrong to think that the balance of power in the Hopkinson family has totally swung behind the Anti-Housing and Development of the Village Campaign camp FOR TWO REASONS:

1. Dad has been delivering Gor May food parcels to the Anti-Anti-Housing and Development of the Village Campaign camp.

2. Vera has crossed the road in the OPPOSITE direction to Harmony. Apparently there was a big overnight situation in the stables.

* CAVE – beware. (Daffodil says it's Latin.)

This is not **OFFICIAL NEWS** yet, but it's reached me that 'the lady who brushes' has driven off with the horse feed merchant – in HIS van.

Anyway, the knock-on effect is that now Vera knows that Grandpa won't be buying 'the lady who brushes' a house.

I was at home this evening, minding my own business and sandwiches because no one else was going to. So I gave Barkley a special treat and told him he could come and sleep on my bed.

I read myself a story, shouted at the owl outside my window to put a sock in it and turned my light off. And I was just about to go to sleep when I heard noises in the attic. It sounded like someone was walking around up there.

I tried to convince myself that it was Moggy having a wander about. But Moggy doesn't walk with a stick and it sounded as if the person in the attic was using one.

My hair stood on end, and so did Barkley's. Our eyes were out on stalks like crabs as we looked at each other.

Then we decided we'd go downstairs and watch some TV till Grandpa and Dad got home. Which they finally did, so I told them on behalf of Barkley and myself what we'd heard.

'That will be Mabel,' he said without a care in the world. As if that was an acceptable answer.

I AM NOT SLEEPING ALONE AGAIN IN THIS HOUSE WITH MABEL AND BARKLEY. FINITO.

CHAPTER 23

THE VCEOC XMAS DUCK RACE

VILLAGE HALL TO THE CHURCH BRIDGE

Mrs Chichester had timed her duck auction for 11 a.m. sharp. Officially it was going to be a seven-duck race for the grand prize.

The owner of the winning plastic duck was set to receive a scented cushion 'generously sponsored by Chichester Interior Design' with the catchy slogan 'A duck isn't just for Christmas' on it.

RESULT OF THE AUCTION:

BABY JESUS DUCK – Officially purchased by Mrs Smartside. She way overpaid for it.

MARY DUCK – purchased by my mum. She is trying to cling on to her seat on the VCEOC by the skin of her coat-tails.

JOSEPH DUCK – purchased by Felicity Snoop. I know what's going on here; Snoop is bigging herself up to hang on to Daffodil as her official best friend.

INNKEEPER (BETHLEHEM) DUCK – reluctantly purchased by the vicar. The bidding for this duck was NOT enthusiastic, so the vicar had to step in after a nasty look from Mrs Chichester.

(As for that innkeeper – what an idiot. This guy has to be the biggest doofus in history – he had a PR penalty kick **DOUBLE-WHOPPER** open-goal opportunity to be able to put a sign up saying jesus was born here. And what did he do? Kick them out into the stables – he must be one of Vinnie's ancestors.)

Then Mrs Chichester pulled a fast one 'to attract a younger audience'. She threw in some contemporary ducks. Mum was **LIVID** – spitting feathers, beaks, entrails, the lot – because she is the resident PR guru (ex) but she HAD NOT been consulted on this.

JUSTIN BEAKER DUCK - Iris was all over him; she says she loves his tight jeans.

DAVID BECKHAMSTEAD DUCK - Wolfe snapped him up; he's nuts about football, and spoiled if you ask me.

PIPPA MIDDLE-CLASS DUCK - Crocus begged her mother to buy that one. She says she wants to be famous when she grows up.

'Excuse you . . . but what do you want to be famous for?' I asked.

'Nothing in particular,' she simpered.

Anyway, after the auction everyone made their way to the river to launch the race – and that's when the stuff that comes out of animals' bottoms hit the fan, as they say in Morocco.

'WHAT HAS HAPPENED TO THE RIVER?'

screeched Mrs Smartside.

It was a fair question – the River Topley had turned into a small puddle, down which no duck of any description was going far. Particularly plastic ones with no engines.

'Oh Lord,' gasped the vicar. But I have a sneaky suspicion he is addressing the wrong culprit.

CHAPTER 24

WATER, WATER, NOT QUITE EVERYWHERE

PANDEMONIUM BROKE OUT ON THE RIVERBANK. MRS SMARTSIDE WAS IN FULL FLOOD – UNLIKE THE RIVER.

'When I find out who is responsible for this . . . That woman in the pub . . . She's no good . . . That family are all trouble . . . wretched Londoners,' she cursed. Her head looked like a recently EXPLODED WATERMELON.

Mum kind of lost it with Mrs Smartside DOUBLE-WHOPPER big time. 'How dare you refer to my family like that . . .? You have no proof of anything . . . and you're a dreadful hypocrite . . . Think you own the place . . . Knickers on your washing line . . . No one wants to see them anyway . . .'

168

I think it's fair to say that Mum's invitation to play bridge with Mrs Smartside has gone west up in flames –

VAMOOSED

– evaporated

– down the Swanee, etc. You get my drift.

WATER NEWS – I didn't think it was the right moment to break it to Mum that her family MIGHT unwittingly be linked to the fluctuations of flow of the River Topley. Third-hand, of course. Not that I had MEANT Vinnie to empty the whole flipping river between the village hall and the church bridge. Idiot.

But time waits for no one in the duck-racing world, and I HAD to be getting down to the start of the Chequers Xmas duck race.

TWO fire engines passed me as I beetled down the lane, wondering all the while if Vinnie had found any water for the river from the church bridge to the Chequers.

Fire engines are never a good sign in my experience. This was no exception!

The Chequers was mayhem, and it didn't take an engineering genius to deduce that the River Topley was now flowing out of the loos, through the bar and into the cellar.

'I've lost a week's supply of Turnip Scallopini with Pomegranate Seeds à la Plancha . . . This is a **DISASTER!**' wailed Dad.

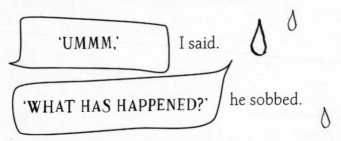

'UMMM,' I said.

'WHAT HAS HAPPENED?' he sobbed.

I slipped out of the pub before anyone started pulling my nails out and generally torturing me for information and went to find you-know-WHO!

Vinnie was standing on the bridge above the church like a drowned urchin, but looking VERY pleased with himself.

Water was pouring the wrong way out of the storm drain and the river between the church and the pub was tidal.

'ALL RIIGHT?' Vinnie asked.

'NICE BIT OF WATER.'

'Excuse you, Vinnie,' I said with my hands firmly on my hips. 'I don't know what you've done, but can you undo it . . . quickly?'

Vinnie waved his hands and shrugged his shoulders like a confused tortoise. 'All riight . . . but I was trying to say . . . You just don't know . . . Water has a mind of its own . . . Storm drains—'

'LA, LA, LA, LA,' I said to Vinnie, not listening.

'IT'S NOTHING TO DO WITH ME, VINNIE . . . JUST TRY TO THINK OF EVERYTHING YOU'VE DONE IN THE LAST FEW HOURS AND DO THE OPPOSITE . . . COMPRENDO?'

And with that Vinnie skulked off like a scolded otter to return normality to the River Topley.

171

And he's now demanding compensation because his ducks are somewhere in the cellar.

Aunt Electra really is very naive when it comes to business matters – I don't think it will be long before Holly Hopkinson Inc. takes over the business side of the pub. Once I have an iPad.

The Chequers Xmas Duck Race was abandoned, which was bad news for Sir Garfield. Some maniac (Aunt Electra – but I'm not naming names) had allowed him to buy every duck in the race, and the cost of the ducks was half the price of a barrel of beer, which was first prize. So Sir Garfield wasn't stupid, thank you very much. But it's all gone banana-shaped on him.

CHAPTER 25

STEVEN SPEEDBERG TURNS UP AT THE CHEQUERS

GRANDPA AND I SPENT THE MORNING WATCHING VINNIE AND LE PRINCE DOING THEIR STUFF. WHEN LE PRINCE STRETCHES OUT, HIS **MASSIVE** BROWN FRAME LOOKS LIKE IT'S GLIDING THROUGH THE AIR LIKE **A STEALTH BOMBER** – READY TO WIPE SOMETHING OUT.

Vinnie did some horse speak when he got off him, which Grandpa and I pretended to understand. We nodded our heads a lot and chewed some grass.

We also went to have a chat with Declan – but he's still having problems with his nerves and he's off his carrots. And Chicken still hasn't returned.

But Grandpa is SO EXCITED about Le Prince that we decided to go and have a slap-up lunch at the Chequers, and check out our resident celebrity chef.

SHOWBIZ NEWS – Aunt Electra was buzzing around the pub like a dragonfly when we got there.

'DARLING . . . YOU'LL NEVER GUESS WHO'S IN THE BAR.'

Aunt Electra gabbled, hair going everywhere and her eyes looking like they were going to head off in different directions to each other.

'LET ME SEE.' I replied.

'IS IT ED SHEAR'UM . . .? NO . . . ANDREW LORD WEBBER . . .? CLOSE . . .? THE QUEEN . . .? NOT TODAY . . . MRS SMARTSIDE . . .? OBVIOUSLY NOT . . . SLINKY DAVE . . .? NOT WITHOUT BOSSY BOSSOM . . . SIR GARFIELD . . . DELIVERING MORE ANIMAL BODY PARTS . . . OR "THE LADY WHO BRUSHES"?'

I asked.

But Aunt Electra just shook her head like an army of ants had pitched camp inside her ears. 'No . . . no . . . no . . . Think bigger, darling,' she said.

'Well, give me a clue, then,' I requested. 'Animal, vegetable or mineral?'

Aunt Electra gasped. 'It's a famous film director . . . In fact, it's the most FAMOUS film director in the WORLD.'

'Well, that doesn't narrow it down much,' I protested.

But we've done films at school, of course, what with Bossy Bossom being an acting **MANIAC**, so I know all of them.

'Is it Woolly Allen . . . Ridley Snott . . . Clint Woodward . . . Stanley Rubik?'

'Honestly, Holly . . . what do they teach you?' Aunt Electra asked. 'He did the film about the fish that ate everyone . . . you know . . .'

'Orca . . . *Finding Nemo* . . . *Flipper* . . . Honestly Aunt Electra, there have been quite a lot of fish films . . .'

'Darling, it was a shark . . . *Jaws* . . . Steven Spielberg, that's who it is.'

'Well, what the **FLIPPING HECK** is he doing here? Don't tell me . . . news has reached Hollywood about Dad's Turnip Scallopini with Pomegranate Seeds à la Plancha?'

'Well, he's ordered the burger, so I don't think so.'

'Maybe he saw Dad on *You Won't Believe Who's Cooking Our Dinner Tonight?* on TV and he's come to sign Dad up for a part in his next blockbuster?'

'I really don't know, Holly . . . It's all too much . . . I really did not expect to be coping with Hollywood greats when I took over being entertainment director of this establishment.'

So I can see straight away what's going on here – SHE wants to be in his next blockbuster and she's going to try to upstage Dad – so I'll have to keep an eye on THAT ONE.

'LEAVE THIS TO ME, AUNT ELECTRA,'

I said.

Anyway, forget blockbusters, I think Steven Speedberg might like to be on Holly Hopkinson's team for the pub quiz tomorrow night.

'BUT, HOLLY ...'

'Not a word, Aunt Electra,' I commanded, zipping up my lips with my fingers by way of visual command. 'This is where the chief executive of Holly Hopkinson Enterprises steps into the ring ... thank you very much.'

Steven Speedberg was sitting in the corner on his own, chomping into a large burger, and if you ask me, he'd put way too much ketchup on his plate. Even Hollywood directors shouldn't have that amount of sugar.

'Hello, Mr Speedberg,' I said. 'How very nice to meet you.'

'I'M SORRY?'

he replied with his mouth full.

'No need to be,' I said, reassuring him, although he didn't look very sorry. So I decided to get my **MAGIC POCKET WATCH** out **DOUBLE-WHOPPER** sharpish. I know what these directors are like – any minute now he might think I'm auditioning for the lead part in his next blockbuster and start shouting 'NEXT'.

'Mr Speedberg . . . would you like to look at my **MAGIC POCKET WATCH** . . .? It's very old,' I said, like a Hollywood star.

'WELL, I'M REALLY VERY—'

'It won't take long,' I assured him, and I started to swing my watch backwards and forwards.

The BIG question was how many verses to give him. On the one hand I didn't want him to go completely Tonto – which film-y types can do – but the pub quiz night was probably going to be a hard sell. So I decided that three verses would do. Plus one because his glasses looked a bit dirty.

'SPIRO, SPERO, SQUIGGLEOUS SCOTCH,
CAST YOUR EYES WHITHER MY WATCH.'

I recited four times nice and slowly.

His little eyes went backwards and forwards quite obediently behind his specs and he went nicely GOGGLE-EYED.

'Mr Speedberg, you will be on my pub quiz team tomorrow night,' I commanded.

'IF YOU SAY SO,' he obliged.

EXCELLENTO, as they say in Norway.

'And you will forget you ever saw this watch.'

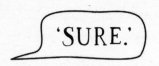

'SURE.'

I got the dose right for once. So I thought, no harm in shooting the breeze for a while. After all, it's not every day that the director of a big fish film drops by.

'So, Mr Speedberg, how long are you hanging out around here?' I asked.

'Well, the thing is . . . I'm looking for some locations for my new blockbuster,' he replied. 'I'm sorry . . . I didn't catch your name.'

'Holly Hopkinson,' I replied, thrusting my hand out. 'Chief executive and founding chairman of Holly Hopkinson Film Location and Places Inc.,' I added.

'Really? You seem a bit young for that sort of thing?'

'Oh no . . . In this part of the world it's a young woman's game.'

'RIGHT . . . WELL, CAN I TELL YOU IN THE STRICTEST CONFIDENCE WHAT I'M LOOKING FOR?'

'MR SPEEDBERG, STRICTEST CONFIDENCE IS WHAT I'M KNOWN FOR . . . I NEVER HAVE A CLUE WHAT'S GOING ON . . . AND IF I DO, PLIERS AND HEATED METAL IRONS CAN'T GET IT OUT OF ME . . . IF YOU GET MY DRIFT.'

And I stuck my tongue out of one side of my mouth and winked at him.

'RIGHT . . . WELL, I NEED LOTS OF OPEN FIELDS . . . SOMEONE WHO CAN RIDE LIKE THEY WERE BORN ON A HORSE . . . AND A BIG, BLACK, BEAUTIFUL HORSE,'

he said.

'BECAUSE I'M GOING TO REMAKE BLACK BEAUTY . . . BUT YOU MUSTN'T TELL ANYONE . . . IT'S A SECRET.'

It was at this point that I realised that Aunt Electra was playing one of her bohemian jokes on me – because he had the worst American accent I've ever heard. Even worse than Bart Simpson's.

She's probably testing me to see if I'm using my **MAGIC POCKET WATCH** properly.

She must think that I'm a right idiot. She's probably hired this clown from the Chipping Topley Theatrical Society. Steven Speedberg indeed. So I decided to show this doofus and Aunt Electra that Holly Hopkinson is not to be goofed around with.

'Excuse you,' I said with my hands on my hips. 'But you might like to know that even Bossy Bossom is better at acting than you are.'

'I BEG YOUR PARDON?'

'Beg away, buster . . . and good day to you,' I said as I stomped out of the bar, sweeping up a rather **DISCOMBOBULATED** Grandpa on my way out.

No one makes a double-whopper doofus of Holly Hopkinson before the cockerel crows three times without getting a slap in the face with a wet kipper.

CHAPTER 26

SPEEDBERG DEBRIEF AT HOME

~~~

SO MUM CAME HOME FOR TEA FROM THE ANTI-HOUSING CAMP, **WHIFFING** LIKE ANYTHING. WHY CAN'T PARENTS WHO GO TO PROTEST CAMPS HAVE BATHS? IT'S ONE THING HAROLD **SMELLING LIKE A POLECAT** – BUT PARENTS ARE QUITE ANOTHER THING.

'Mum . . . are you going to have a scrub before we have tea?' I asked.

'Oh, Holly . . . where is your passion? I am devoting myself to saving the green fields around Lower Goring.'

'Don't you start, Mum . . . You're beginning to sound like Aunt Electra . . . You're meant to be a PR guru in London . . . not a **BOHEMIAN LUNATIC** smelling of campfires . . . and it has to stop . . . because you are all freaking Declan out.'

'OH . . . I THOUGHT AUNT ELECTRA WAS MRS PERFECT.'

'SHE CERTAINLY IS NOT . . . SHE PLAYED A TRICK ON ME IN THE PUB TODAY . . . SHE TOLD ME THAT STEVEN SPEEDBERG, THE FAMOUS HOLLYWOOD DIRECTOR, WAS IN THE PUB AND I THOUGHT HE'D COME TO SIGN DAD UP FOR SOME BLOCKBUSTER FILM . . . AND GUESS WHAT?'

'WELL, I'VE NEVER HEARD OF A FILM DIRECTOR CALLED SPEEDBERG . . . ARE YOU SURE YOU DON'T MEAN . . .?'

'WHAT I MEAN IS THAT HE WAS A FLIPPING ACTOR FROM CHIPPING TOPLEY.'

'WELL, WHY WOULD AUNT ELECTRA TRICK YOU LIKE THAT . . .? I SHALL HAVE A WORD WITH HER.'

Anyway, I was about to get my **MAGIC POCKET WATCH** out to hypnotise Mum and order her to shut her anti-housing camp down when Aunt Electra and Dad came crashing through the door, behaving like they'd just won a cake-off and eaten all the icing sugar.

'Holly . . . you are a legend,' Dad shouted, picking me up and whirling me around.

'You're learning, Holly,' said Aunt Electra, giving me a knowing glance.

'It's not nice to tease Holly . . . Stop it at once,' Mum demanded.

'DARLING . . . HASN'T SHE TOLD YOU . . .? HOLLY HAS PERSUADED THE GREATEST FILM DIRECTOR IN THE WORLD TO JOIN HER TEAM IN THE QUIZ TOMORROW NIGHT,'

Aunt Electra said, chortling.

'WE'LL HAVE A PACKED HOUSE.'

'SO IT WASN'T A JOKE?' I asked.

185

'He's coming and the whole of Chipping Topley has heard . . . We're booked out tomorrow night,' Dad said in his 'celebrity chef' voice.

'I'm going to do a set menu so everyone has to try my Turnip Scallopini with Pomegranate Seeds à la Plancha.'

— BREAKING NEWS —

Ten minutes later the phone rang and guess who was on the end of it? Only Mrs Smartside. Mum put the phone on loudspeaker.

'Sally, dear . . . we're all grown-ups . . . We can put that little misunderstanding at the duck race behind us, can't we . . .? I was thinking . . . it does seem awfully silly to have the VCEOC quiz and the pub quiz on the same night . . . Why don't we combine both of them . . .? The village hall could fit everyone in.'

'Well, it's not really my department . . . Electra is running the pub quiz . . . and I'm QUITE busy organising the anti-housing camp that YOU asked me to,' Mum replied.

'Sally, you're doing such a good job . . . The whole village is SOOO grateful,' purred Mrs Smartside down the phone.

'More like HALF the village,' said Mum sardonically*.

'Well, perhaps you could have a word with that woman for me?' enquired Mrs Smartside.

'Well, she's right here, so I'll just pass you over,' replied Mum, running her fingers across her throat and pulling a very undignified face.

'What can I do for you, darling?' asked Aunt Electra.

'Oh, Electra . . . I was thinking it would make much more sense to combine our quizzes . . . bring everyone together . . . Christmas . . . festive spirit . . . blah . . . blah.'

* SARDONICALLY – not sucking up hot air.

187

'Good idea, darling,' chirped Aunt Electra triumphantly. 'Bring your lot to the Chequers . . . with your celebrities, of course . . . Bye.'

And with that Aunt Electra cut off the phone call and pirouetted around the kitchen like a mad spaniel trying to bite its own tail.

So I sent an URGENT text to Aleeshaa on my smart mobile phone.

HI, ALEESHAA. YOU WON'T BELIEVE THIS BUT STEVEN SPEEDBERG IS IN MY QUIZ TEAM TOMORROW NIGHT – CAN YOU COME TOO? 😊

She replied straight away.

HEY, GIRL . . . RANDOM . . . 😄 HOPE IT DOESN'T GET STRUCK BY LIGHTNING. BE COOL.

I may have been a little rude to Steven Speedberg.

CHAPTER 27

THE DAY OF THE PUB QUIZ

SO IT DIDN'T TAKE LONG FOR THE
WAGONS TO START CIRCLING ONCE THE
SPEEDBERG QUIZ NEWS HAD REACHED
CHICHESTER FABRICS AND CHICHESTER
INTERIOR DESIGN (ONLY MRS CHICHESTER
KNOWS THE DIFFERENCE BETWEEN THEM).

As soon as dawn broke – or maybe about mid-morning – guess who came bumping down Grandpa's drive looking for their pound of flesh (which in this case is a golden ticket to be on MY celebrity quiz team)?

YES.

My ex-best friend (official) and the co-chairperson of the Anti-Housing and Development of the Village Campaign (her mother).

'Oh, Holly dear . . . is your mother in?' Mrs Chichester asked.

'In where, Mrs Chichester?' I asked.

At which point Vera appeared from the middle of nowhere like she's a secret agent. And Mrs Chichester started muttering to her, doing that adult thing when they think children can't hear what they're saying.

'That child . . . **IMPOSSIBLE** . . . preconscious*,' babbled Mrs Chichester.

But what she has forgotten is that Vera has crossed the road and joined the Anti-Anti-Housing campaign. So they are NO LONGER fleas in a sack together.

* PRECONSCIOUS –
young person knowing
what someone is thinking
before they think it.

Vera got pretty angry with Mrs Chichester and then VAMOOSED back inside.

So Mrs Chichester cut to the chase. 'Holly, dear . . . Daffodil was wondering if she could be in your team this evening?' Mrs Chichester gushed like a FLUSHING BOG.

Daffodil was skulking in the back of the car, not moving a muscle like Barkley does when he's watching food programmes on TV.

'Well,' I replied, 'I thought Daffodil would be on Felicity Snoop's team . . . seeing as they're best friends now.'

'OH NO . . . GOOD LORD, NO . . . FELICITY SNOOP . . . I DON'T THINK SO . . .'

gabbled Mrs Chichester.

Daffodil was rapidly disappearing out of view.

'The thing is, I've promised all my own best friends a place on my team . . . so I think I'm a bit full . . . but I'll see what I can do . . . if Daffodil definitely isn't Felicity Snoop's best friend.'

'SHE IS NOT,'

Mrs Chichester growled.

Daffodil's head reappeared and she shook it compliantly like a **WILD ANIMAL** conceding defeat after a fight rather than getting eaten.

—— **BREAKING NEWS** ——
IT LOOKS LIKE DAFFODIL CHICHESTER IS OFFICIALLY MY BEST FRIEND AGAIN.

CHAPTER 28

MIDDAY NEWS

THE NEXT PERSON WHO CAME
CRASHING DOWN THE DRIVE TO
THE FARMYARD WAS ONLY SLINKY
DAVE. AND I HAD A FEELING **WHY.**

Now that I'm **OFFICIALLY** in the film business, I shouldn't wonder if Slinky Dave isn't going to offer me the bus as my official transport.

'Someone seems to be very popular this morning, young lady,' observed Grandpa, looking up from his *Racing Post*. 'I wonder why?'

Grandpa doesn't really get celebrity status unless they're jockeys, so I didn't bother to wear my vocal cords out explaining that Holly Hopkinson Film Location and Places Inc. was about to smash through a glass window into the big time.

But I had called this one wrong. Because guess who popped out of the bus like an expectant frog and was all over me like one of Vera's chocolate mousses?

- YES. -

Bossy Bossom, of course.

The same Bossom who roasted me in my school report, I didn't remind myself. Because I've moved on from that and am not even thinking about it.

'Holly . . . Holly . . . Holly . . . How lovely to see you . . . you clever girl . . . I mean . . .'

'Hello, Miss Bossom . . . What a surprise . . . And you must be so busy getting ready for the quiz . . . Both quizzes, in fact?'

'Yes . . . Well, I've managed to get everyone to agree to combine the two . . . Yes, in the pub . . . of course,' Bossy babbled.

'Well, that's good . . . So what can I do you for, Miss Bossom?' I asked severely.

'Er . . . I hear you have a special guest on your team . . . Just wondering if you could introduce us . . .? I was thinking . . . he might like to audition me . . .'

So I gave it to her straight – because that's the way it is in Hollywood. And I made it very clear that plenty of questions about fish films wouldn't do her prospects any harm.

Half an hour later one visitor too many came trotting down towards the farm –

YOU **WILL NOT**

BELIEVE THIS –

it was Felicity flipping Snoop, bold as grass on her perfect pony.

It was the camel that finally ate the straw.

'Vera . . . please inform Felicity Snoop that I am not available,' I requested of Grandpa's reinstated underwear keeper as I skedaddled off to the Bogey Club headquarters for some peace and quiet.

CHAPTER 29

THE ACTUAL DAY
OF THE PUB QUIZ

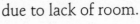

EVEN THOUGH WE WERE VERY
EARLY FOR THE OFFICIAL STARTING
TIME, THE CHEQUERS WAS BURSTING
AT ITS SEAMS WHEN WE ARRIVED.

Beanstalk was livid, totally **LIVID**, when Vinnie
had to explain to her it was a no horse or pony night
due to lack of room.

And someone was outside the front door taking
a photograph. I think he was from the roundabout
above Chipping Topley.

With my business hat on I officially decided to let Daffodil join my team – because she is the smartest kid in my class by a long way, and I want to WIN. But here is the **BREAKING NEWS** – I have also invited Vinnie to be on my team.

Yes, I know what you're thinking... Why would anyone want Vinnie on their quiz team? Well, I have two reasons:

1. OPTICS (AS WE SAY IN THE TRADE) – on reflection, I'm a bit short of official best friends, so I need to big up Vinnie as the BEST best friend ever. Which will be fine as long as Vinnie and Daffodil don't discuss best friends. (Which is unlikely as Vinnie doesn't discuss anything with anyone.)

2. **BUSINESS** – remember Steven Speedberg told me he was looking for 'someone who can ride like they were born on a horse'? Of course I know the very person. So I've got Vinnie on the same sort of contract that The Cool are on. If Vinnie is going to make it big in Hollywood, no one else is going to be eating his lunch except me, pardon my French.

MORE **BREAKING NEWS** – blow me down with a ton of bricks, guess who was already at our table, waving at me like a lunatic?

YES.

STEVE.

You'd think Hollywood directors would be a bit cooler than that, wouldn't you?

'Over here, Holly,' he was shouting. 'I've got our table.'

Everyone from Chipping Topley and Lower Goring was jammed in by the time Bossy Bossom started ringing her bell, even Sir Garfield, Dad's butcher friend, who was on Vince's team. Who would have put them down as a pub quiz types?

Glaring across the room at them were Mrs Smartside and 'Interior Charmian', looking like a couple of overfed chocolate Labradors about to pounce on a tin of cheap dog food. And they had muscled in on a table near the front.

Dad and Aunt Electra had forgotten about security and what with the anti-housing and the anti-anti-housing brigades all being crammed into the same place, there was no guarantee that this wouldn't turn nasty if Miss Bossom lit a few bonfires. And I couldn't help but notice that Felicity Snoop's team was one short.

I chuckled slightly nervously. 'I hope you didn't mind my little joke yesterday, Sir Steve.'

'Er . . . there's no "sir".' He replied in his 'slightly miffed' voice.

'Well, don't worry about that, Steve,' I reassured him. 'Because the queen is an old mate of mine . . . so we can soon get that sorted out . . . After all, Ridley's got one and he never did anything as good as your fish film.'

Steve looked at me with his grumpy face, but I'm going to forgive him because he's from California and they're all a bit like that there.

'Yes . . . well, I'm glad we've cleared that up, Steve . . . Now I want to talk to you about locations before the quiz starts . . . Just look at my MAGIC POCKET WATCH.'

But just as I was about to get him GOGGLE-EYED up comes Daffodil in one of her Mrs Chichester dresses, being a FLIBBERTIGIBBET all over Steve like he was a cheap suit. And then the flipping quiz started.

CHAPTER 30

THE VILLAGE AND CHEQUERS (OFFICIAL) PUB QUIZ

SPOILER ALERT – I JUST DON'T
KNOW WHAT MISS BOSSOM WAS THINKING
WHEN SHE MADE UP THE QUIZ – BUT IT
WAS A TOTAL DISASTER.

This is how it all BLEW UP.

'Attention, please, lords, ladies and gentlemen, and directors,' Bossy announced with a bit of a nervous titter added in. 'Shall we get started?'

Thankfully the first part of the quiz was written answers only.

But here's the **CELEBRITY NEWS** – Steve couldn't answer any of the questions AT ALL. Which was very embarrassing for me, seeing as I invited him. I think the problem was:

1. The questions weren't in Californian, so he didn't understand them.

2. Film directors don't know much about stuff.

3. The questions weren't about fish films.

Of course I was TOO busy as team captain, holding things together, to have time to answer them.

SO HERE ARE A FEW OF THE LUNATIC QUESTIONS:

Q What is an alektorophobic afraid of? *(Answer – chickens.)*

Q What is a hippopotomonstrosesquippedaliophobic afraid of? *(Answer – long words – very funny indeed.)*

Q What is someone doing to you if they bumfuzzle you? *(Answer – confusing you; so you could say this is a bumfuzzling quiz, pardon my French.)*

Q If someone is rambunctious, what are they? *(Answer – someone with a lot of energy who tends to cause trouble – and we all know people like that, thank you very much.)*

Q What is arctophily? *(Answer – collecting teddy bears.)*

Q What is philematology? *(Answer – the art of kissing, so Slinky Dave is responsible for that question.)*

Then I had to put in an **OFFICIAL** complaint because the Pony Club (II) team – Wolfe, Gaspar and Tiger – either a) developed very weak bladders or b) were looking up the answers in the loos on their phones.

Then we came to the shouting-out answers section – where we were big favourites obviously – but it went from bad to ugly, and Steve just fell to pieces. They clearly don't have to work under this sort of pressure in **HOLLYWOOD**.

Bossy served us up a couple of DOUBLE-WHOPPER doddle fish film questions for starters. So we should have been off to a flying start.

Q Who starred in *Orca the Killer Whale*? Was it **A)** Richard Harris **B)** Ronald Reagan or **C)** Richard Nixon?

'Who is it, Steve?' I asked in my 'shushed' voice.

But all I got was: 'I'm not answering that one . . . He copied my film . . . Should never have been released . . . It was a scandal.'

'Flipping heck, Steve. Just answer the question,' I begged.

But he was having none of it.

And Felicity Snoop's depleted team grabbed the point. 'Richard Harris,' she shouted – although I think she had an iPad under the table.

Steve was no better at the next question.

Q Who was Nemo's friend in *Finding Nemo*? Was it **A)** Doris **B)** Dory or **C)** Dave?

'It's "b",' whispered Daffodil.

'Shhh,' I hissed in my 'snake' voice. 'This is Steve's department.'

'That film shouldn't have won so many awards . . . It was ridiculous . . . Mine was much better . . .' Steve bawled. And then he stood up and just flounced off.

'Excuse you . . . where are you going?' I asked.

'The Blue Boar in Chipping Topley,' was his shameless reply.

WHAT A DRAMA QUEEN.

So I had to **DOUBLE-WHOPPER** spit-spot if total **DISASTER** was to be avoided.

I NEEDED HIM TO LOOK AT MY

MAGIC POCKET WATCH.

'No trouble, Steve,' I assured him. 'My driver can drop us off.'

'Oh . . . I'd forgotten my limo isn't here . . . Well, that would be good . . . OK.'

So with that I gave a loud Vinnie-style wolf whistle in Dave's direction. And he had the school bus round by the front door in a jiffy.

'At your service, sir,' Dave said – a little too unctuously, if you ask me.

'That's more like it,' I heard him mutter.

So I decided to play him at Dave's game. If that's what he wants to be called until I've got him a sir, why didn't he just say so?

'Sir, please would you be so kind to look at my **MAGIC POCKET WATCH?**' I asked in MY unctuous voice.

'Hey . . . That looks cool . . . Where did you get that?'

'Just watch it very carefully, please,' I unctuated*.

His eyes went backwards and forwards like an obedient cuckoo clock as I recited five verses of **SPIRO, SPERO.**

'Tomorrow we are going to find you a location for your new blockbuster film *Black Beauty* . . . Although, just to be clear, can we decide whether it's going to involve fish or not?'

'No fish . . . What is it with you and fish?' he harrumphed. Well, he's one to talk.

'We are also going to find you a black horse and someone who was born on one.'

* UNCTUATED
– greasing up to people while you do grammar.

'Yeah . . . sure, kid . . . Just so long as you deliver . . . And for the last time . . . NO FISH.'

NOTE TO SELF: I'm beginning to think that Hollywood directors think life is all about them. And they're rubbish at pub quizzes.

CHAPTER 31

CRACK-OF-DAWN BREAKING NEWS

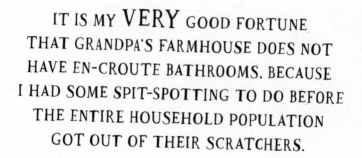

IT IS MY **VERY** GOOD FORTUNE
THAT GRANDPA'S FARMHOUSE DOES NOT
HAVE EN-CROUTE BATHROOMS, BECAUSE
I HAD SOME SPIT-SPOTTING TO DO BEFORE
THE ENTIRE HOUSEHOLD POPULATION
GOT OUT OF THEIR SCRATCHERS.

I didn't know what the thing I was looking for looked like – but I knew I'd know it when I saw it, because it's not an everyday condiment* for most people – definitely not Grandpa anyway – so I could save myself a bad experience by poking around in his private bathroom cupboards.

> * CONDIMENT –
> a sauce or spice
> that people say nice
> things about.

I didn't even want to think about what HE might have stored away – stuff like: **FALSE TEETH**, out-of-date **ATHLETIC FOOT** powder, the tweezers that he's lost to pull hairs out of

 his nose, earwax removers (past their use-by date years ago), postcards that he thinks he's hiding from Vera but actually she knows all about them.

So I crept down the corridor as quietly as I could to Mum and Dad's bathroom, which given the creakiness of the floorboards was about as silent as a runaway orchestra playing *Peter and the Wolf* full blast.

Mum was definitely a non-runner for what I was looking for – but Dad might have a guilty secret on this front.

So I had a good rummage through his toilet bag (I know – rude word – but us memoir writers have to go with words that Americans will understand).

He had all the usual stuff in there: toothpaste . . . a lemon (not sliced) . . . a comb (quite a lot of dandruff on it) . . . Mum's shampoo (so that's something  she won't be happy about – I'll be keeping that one up my sleeve for a rainy day), a CORKSCREW and a small hammer.

Why on earth would you have a **HAMMER** in your washbag? . . . There's a limit to how often I can use the other word, if you please!

But what I was looking for was NOT present, so I moved on to the room that Aunt Electra shares with Harmony to do her bohemian ablutions – usually accompanied by some bad singing, I should add for the record.

ENVIRONMENTAL NEWS –

there should be a by-law preventing small children and domestic pets from going into Aunt Electra's bathroom. WHAT A CARRY-ON.

The place looked like a prison riot had got out of hand — and it properly ponged of her 'candyfloss' aftershave, or scent, or whatever it is — air un-freshener?

I was on the verge of passing out as I scrabbled my way through various powders, mascaras, body mist, paint, something that looked like a torture weapon, tonics, a small bottle of gin and a clove of garlic?

THEN I FINALLY FOUND

WHAT I WAS LOOKING FOR.

BINGO TOPLEY,

as they say in Russia.

CHAPTER 32

TRANSPORT FOR MR SPEEDBERG

GIVEN THAT MY **RIDICULOUS** PARENTS ARE COMPLETELY UNRELIABLE RIGHT NOW IN THE TRANSPORT DEPARTMENT, WITH THE HELP OF MY MAGIC POCKET WATCH I HAVE PUT SLINKY DAVE AND THE SCHOOL BUS ON A NO-HOURS CONTRACT.

First stop was Vince's farm to deliver the bottle from Aunt Electra's washbag to Vinnie.

'Vinnie, you will need to spit-spot,' I said. 'Because Slinky Dave and I will be back here with Mr Speedberg in a cat's whisper.'

'All riight . . . but—'

'No buts, Vinnie . . . It's man or mouse time,' I reminded him.

The last person I needed mooching about while I was trying to turn his farm into a film set was Vince, so I told him Grandpa needed him lickety-split down at his farm to get the tractor going – it would take them ages to realise that somehow the spark plugs had come loose.

Mr Speedberg was clicking his heels and raring to go on the pavement outside the Blue Boar when we rocked up.

'Buckle up, sir . . . Wonderment awaits your delectation,' I OFFICIALLY announced in my 'blockbuster' film location voice.

'I hope this isn't a wild-goose chase,' he answered grumpily.

As I had rather suspected that he might, Mr Speedberg noticed the anti-housing and anti-anti-housing camps strewn either side of the entrance to Vince's farm.

'Hey . . . Kind of what is going on here?' he enquired.

'Oh . . . just a slight local disagreement . . . but it will be over shortly . . . Nothing to worry about.'

'So not the unions . . .¿ I don't want any trouble with unions.'

'No . . . no . . . We don't have any trouble with people joining up around here,' I reassured him.

Thankfully the demo camps passed quickly out of his mind as Slinky Dave shuddered the bus to a halt next to the 'grass-chewing' gate.

The **world-famous** director got out of the bus and admired the view across Vince's farm towards the village. 'Oh my gosh . . . This is beautiful,' he simpered.

'Holly Hopkinson Film Location and Places Inc. never fails,' I said smugly. 'You could run the Charge of the Light Brigade up that valley over there,' I added, getting a bit runaway with myself.

'But that doesn't happen in *Black Beauty*,' he pointed out.

'We never say never at Holly Hopkinson Film Location and Places Inc.,' I reminded him. 'Anyway, it's funny you should mention *Black Beauty* . . . Oh, look . . . here he comes now.'

And, bang on cue, Vinnie and Le Prince appeared on the horizon, did the rearing-up bit that black horses always do in the adverts, then they galloped up to where we were leaning on the gate and screeched to a halt in a very dramatic fashion.

'Hey . . . He looks like a beauty . . . What a horse . . . and what a rider.'

'Meet Vinnie . . . who was born on a horse . . . and Le Prince . . . otherwise regularly referred to by independent passersby as Black Beauty,' I said with a flourish.

Vinnie had developed a bit of a tan since I'd dropped Aunt Electra's bottle off earlier that morning.

AND THEN DOUBLE-WHOPPER

DISASTER STRUCK –

IT STARTED TO

FLIPPING WELL RAIN.

It was just a few spots to start with – and then it deluged down. It was like standing under a power shower on volume ten.

And, streak by streak, Black Beauty turned back into Brown Beauty before our very eyes as Aunt Electra's hair dye washed off.

Vinnie looked rather peculiar too – a bit like a human zebra. Most of the hair dye had somehow ended up on his face.

MY WORLD WAS MELTING UNDER
MY FEET LIKE AN ICE CREAM ON
A BOILING-HOT DAY.

CHAPTER 33

THE MAGIC POCKET WATCH GETS THE JOB DONE

I WAS **NOT** HAVING VICTORY
SNATCHED FROM THE JAWS OF
DEFEAT, SO I HAD TO MOVE FAST.

'Just look at my lovely **MAGIC POCKET WATCH**, sir,' I commanded. 'Backwards and forwards, forwards and backwards . . . That's right.'

I decided to stick with four verses; they'd worked last time and he had a fair bit of rain on his glasses.

'SPIRO, SPERO, SQUIGGLEOUS SCOTCH,
CAST YOUR EYES WHITHER MY WATCH!'

'Mr Speedberg, you and I are going to have a chat about this magnificent location . . . and at the end of it you are going to choose Vince's farm to film your *Black Beauty* blockbuster on . . . and Vinnie will be the stunt rider and Le Prince will be Black Beauty once we've made him black again . . . **COMPRENDO?**'

'Yes, Holly . . . Hey, that will be great . . . but we'd better get some better dye.'

'All right . . . No wise cracks . . . Thank you very much . . . And I will be Vinnie and Le Prince's agent.'

'Sure thing.'

'Oh . . . One other thing . . . The Chequers will supply all the food for the film set.'

'It's a done deal, Holly . . . Put it there.'

And with that he spat on his hand and went to shake mine. These film directors really do have some revolting habits.

so it turns out that although the world-famous director has dirty glasses, he doesn't miss a trick.

'Hey . . . What's that over there?' he asked, pointing towards Mrs Smartside's orchard. 'Is it like a windsock . . . We have those back home.'

'Er . . . no . . . That's Mrs Smartside's underwear department . . . flapping all over the place.'

That's all you need when you're trying to get a film location deal, thank you very much. Because if you think about it, that's not something you generally see in the background of respectable films like *Black Beauty*. But sometimes oversized underwear has a silver lining.

'Hey . . . I've got an idea . . . We need to build like a kind of Olde Worlde film set village where Black Beauty lives . . . We could use that to block out that terrible washing line.'

'Er . . . how big does that village need to be?'

'About a dozen houses . . . cute little things . . . real pretty.'

'Would ten do?' I asked, using my thinking cap.

'Yeah . . . that'll do.'

'Well, why don't you build ten real houses . . .? Then they won't blow over if we get one of those storms that we get around here . . . normally when people are right in the middle of putting up a film set. James Bond's lot got washed all the way to Chipping Topley one year.'

'Hey . . . That's a great idea . . . Will they allow that?'

'Mr Speedberg, that is what you are paying "we never say never" Holly Hopkinson Film Location and Places Inc. for.'

At this rate Holly Hopkinson is going to have iPads coming out of her ears.

WHAT COULD POSSIBLY GO WRONG?

CHAPTER 34

OLIVE BOWL TIME

TODAY IS OFFICIALLY OLIVE BOWL TIME* FOR HOLLY HOPKINSON. BUT I WOULD LIKE TO MAKE IT **OFFICIAL NEWS** THAT MY MOTIVATION FOR CLEARING UP THIS HOUSING DISPUTE THAT VINCE KICKED OFF IN THE FIRST PLACE IS PURELY ON BEHALF OF DECLAN, AND **NOT IPADS**, BECAUSE IF THIS STAND-OFF CONTINUES FOR MUCH LONGER, HE WILL HAVE **STRESSED** HIMSELF INTO LITTLE MORE THAN CLEAR SOUP. AND CLEAR SOUP DOES NOT WIN **ROSETTES** AND **PRIZES** AT THE CHEQUERS XMAS PONY RACE.

---

* **OLIVE BOWL TIME** – biblical reference to when people used to sit round fires and eat olives off branches together to sort out arguments. In modern times jars and bowls have become more popular.

So while Grandpa, Vince and me were leaning over the gate watching Le Prince and Vinnie chomp some grass (Declan is too distressed to even come out and eat grass – but at least Chicken has returned home), I pulled Vince to one side for a little chat.

'Have you seen my watch, Vince?' I asked.

'Ah.'

'Good, can you just watch it very carefully for me?'

'Ah.'

So I gave Vince five verses of **sPiRo, sPeRo** – the same dose that inspired him to put in for planning permission for a hundred houses rather than the ONE I suggested for Stickly.

'Vince – you are going to go back to the council and you will drop the number of houses you want to build to ten nice Olde Worlde houses –

DO YOU UNDERSTAND?'

'Ah,' said a properly GOGGLE-EYED Vince, nodding.

'And, Vince, in the event that Steven Speedberg comes along and says he wants to rent YOUR farm as a film set and build those ten houses for you, you are going to say YES. **COMPRENDO?**'

'Ah.'

'And you will let Stickly's family live in one of them.'

'Ah.'

'And, Vince, once all the housing demonstrators have gone away you will pay me a fee equivalent to half an iPad for my services in this matter – no questions answered.'

'Ah.' Vince nodded again.

I like doing **GOGGLE-EYEING** with simple folk like Vince who don't muck you about.

Next stop was the Anti-Housing and Development of the Village Campaign camp to have a little chat with my mother. She had been cooking breakfast for some of her diehards and was whiffing of bacon.

'Good morning, Mum,' I said. 'How goes it?'

'Very well, thank you, neutral Holly,' she replied coolly.

'I've brought you a bowl of olives from the store cupboard,' I said, using my full diplomatic skills.

But she didn't seem to have her attitude adjusted much by the olives, so that's the last time I'm bothering with carting that lot all over the place, leaking into my pocket as well, thank you very much.

'Look at my lovely watch, Mum,' I commanded.

'Very nice, Holly, but I haven't got time to hang around looking at watches.'

So I quickly gave Mum four verses before she knew what had hit her, which is one more than her normal dosage, because she is CLEARLY in a rather feisty, protesting mood at the moment.

'Mum, it's time you went back to work in London.'

'YES, HOLLY . . . BUT–'

'So if Vince drops his planning application to ten Olde Worlde houses, you will call off the dogs, straighten out Mrs Smartside and her flipping washing line and the lot of you will VAMOOSE.'

'Yes, Holly . . . that would be a huge victory for the working-class commuters of Little Goring.'

'Well, that's settled . . . Oh, just one small thing . . . I will need a small payment for my trouble . . . equivalent to the cost of half an iPad . . . which I'm sure your computers can rustle up between them while they're goofing around on the train?'

'Yes, Holly . . . that seems very reasonable.'

'See you later, Mum . . . Love you,' I said, blowing a kiss. I'm not getting closer than that until she's had a double-whopper bath.

The next bit was the tricky part – because after I'd crossed the road to the anti-anti camp I had to get halfway up a tree to talk to Harold.

'Good morning, Harold, I've brought you a jar of olives,' I said in my 'band manager' voice.

'Great . . . I'm starving . . . that smell of bacon over the road is doing my head in.'

'Good . . . well, while you're scoffing those olives, look at my MAGIC POCKET WATCH, Harold.'

'Hey, that's cool, little sis . . . Any more food?'

'As much food as you like . . . as long as you look at my MAGIC POCKET WATCH . . . Backwards . . . forwards . . . forwards . . . backwards.'

Harold was looking a bit weak and GOOFY, so I only gave him three verses of SPIRO, SPERO. I didn't want him

falling out of
the tree.

'Harold, if only ten Olde Worlde house are built on Vince's farm, I can get those **LUNATICS** over the road with Mum to back off . . . and one of them will definitely be for Stickly's family . . . so you are going to persuade your lot that this is a good deal . . . and break up this camp before Declan melts into thin air.'

'Yes, Holly.' **'EXCELLENTO.'**

I got a text from Aleeshaa this evening.

HEY. I JUST SAW THE STORY – YOU REALLY DID HAVE SPIELBERG ON YOUR QUIZ TEAM 😲 LET ME KNOW WHEN HE'S NEXT IN TOWN.

(She should turn her auto spell check off – you've got to get people's names right when you're in the movie business.)

So I replied:

HI. WE SURE DID – AND NO LIGHTNING. 😲 SUPER BUSY WITH MOVIES DOWN HERE.

It will NOT do Aleeshaa any harm to know the countryside isn't as uncool as she thinks – thank you very much.

CHAPTER 35

MUM GETS A CALL FROM STEVEN SPEEDBERG

SO FOR THE FIRST TIME SINCE MUM
AND HARMONY WENT OFF PROTESTING
AGAINST UNION JACK PORKER'S HAPPY
ENGLISH PORK PIES AT HAPPY
FARM, THE FAMILY HOPKINSON ALL
HAD BREAKFAST TOGETHER.

Grandpa was VERY happy with his noggin buried in the *Racing Post*, and no pestering from Vera ironing his underpants and making 'Northern' noises.

Dad was flicking his way through Mrs Beeton's cookbook, looking for tips on the right exotic nosh for a troop of Italian Morris dancers who've booked into the Chequers for their Xmas dinner.

PUDDING NEWS – you'll never guess what Dad's going to give them for pudding?

PUDDING DE CERVEILLES ET LANGUE

INGREDIENTS:

4 SHEEP TONGUES

4 SHEEP BRAINS

1 HARD-BOILED EGG (SLICED)

1 SHALLOT (FINELY CHOPPED)

1 TEASPOON PARSLEY

10 TEASPOONS FLOUR

SALT AND PEPPER

SOME SUET PASTE

* DO NOT LET YOUR PARENTS
TRY TO MAKE THIS AT HOME.

My NEXT task is to un-exotic Dad's cooking double-whopper quick time before he makes the NEWS for the WRONG reasons.

Aunt Electra was doing her raw-eggs-and-Worcester-sauce-swallowing act, accompanied by noises that could have been a cow passing wind.

Harold, who had been well and truly scrubbed down outside in the farmyard when he came down from his tree, was talking about calling an **OFFICIAL** band practice session of The Cool, so he hasn't thought the **BOGGLE-EYES** problem through. Idiot — typical boy.

Luckily for him Harmony had the food mixer going and didn't hear him; otherwise his head might have been included in her 'green juice'.

Mum was last down, and she looked spit-spot when she surfaced. No whiff of the anti camp hanging about, but no **GURU** London clothes on either; she looked like a cat ready to pounce on a mouse. And she did! On ME, THANK you very much.

'Right, everyone,' she said. 'Now that *I* have sorted out the housing debacle, it's time to get my family shipshape. So to show that there are no grudges or hard feelings about who was on which side, I shall start with Neutral Holly,' Mum announced.

'So, Holly . . . let's start with an up-to-date SWOT analysis of where you are, shall we?'

'Excuse you, Mum . . . I can't even remember what "SWOT" stands for.'

'Of course you can, Holly,' Mum said, still on my case. '"S" for Strengths, "W" for Weaknesses, "O" for Opportunities and "T" for Threats . . .'

'How about "T" for treats?' I suggested.

This SWOT nonsense was NOT my plan, I can tell you, but just as I was coming up with a threat to threaten Mum with, guess what happened?

BIG NEWS BROKE ON THE TV – AND GUESS WHOSE FACE APPEARED ON THE SCREEN?

YES.

MUM'S!

Even Mum had to break wind and stop her SWOT nonsense.

'TURN IT UP, HOLLY, **TURN IT UP,**

everyone shouted.

'The authorities have announced that Union Jack Porker's Happy English Pork Pies have been shut down because their pies contain horse meat from industrial parks,' the newsreader said. Then they started showing the film of Mum being marched off by the cops at the protest.

NO GRASS

'Sally Hopkinson was a lone voice in alerting the world to this scandal, and lost her job as a result,' the newsreader continued.

And then our kitchen went

RONCO-BONCO.

'Mum . . . you, like, sooo did it!' shouted Harmony. 'You, like, showed the faith.'

'Yes . . . well done, Mum,' I added quickly.

'FANTASTICEROO.'

'Well, I never,' Mum said. 'It's all thanks to—'

And just as I thought she was going to say 'HOLLY' she flipping well said 'Harmony'.

So I was the only person in our kitchen not going bonkero when the phone rang.

'HELLO . . . this is the Hopkinson residence . . . What can I do you for?' I enquired.

'Hey . . . I'd like to speak to the great Sally Hopkinson, please,' said an annoying-sounding American voice.

'To whom might she be speaking to if I go and get her . . .? Which is not definite,' I added.

'This is Mr Spe . . . berg's office, ma'am.'

'Excuse YOU,' I replied. 'I think you'll find it's Holly Hopkinson he wants to talk to, if I'm not mistaken.'

'No, ma'am . . . It's definitely the famous Sally Hopkinson that he wants to speak with.'

'Talk to . . . in English . . . not speak with,' I corrected.

'Is Sally Hopkinson available at this time, ma'am?' the human robot persisted.

'Have you ever seen my **MAGIC POCKET WATCH?**' I asked, not thinking that one through.

'EXCUSE ME?'

'You aren't,' I replied. 'But I'll get my mother . . . Good day to you.'

'The phone's for you, Mum . . . It's MY FRIEND Steve, by the way. I have no idea why he wants to speak to you.'

Mum thought I was kidding, but she picked up the phone anyway. Then her mouth fell open. 'Yes . . . Really . . . Well, that's nice of you to say so . . . WHAT . . . are you serious . . .?

Oh my gosh . . . I'd love to . . . Tomorrow . . . in London . . . OK . . . See you then . . . Thank you, sir.'

'Blimey,' said Mum when the call ended. 'I've just been hired by the most famous film director in the world to do his worldwide PR . . . He says I'm his hero for standing up to corrupt corporate pie makers.'

I AM VERY PROUD OF MY MOTHER – although obviously a little disappointed not to have been offered the job myself – which I would have turned down, of course.

Guess who also rang Mum?

YES.

Mum's old PR firm – their people are in so much doo-doo for helping to promote Union Jack Porker's Happy English Pork Pies at Happy Farm that they now need someone to HELP THEM with their own PR.

Mum told their people that she is rather busy right now – THANK YOU
VERY MUCH.

CHAPTER 36

MUM GETS BACK FROM LONDON

HERE IS THE **_LONDON NEWS_**, AS REPORTED BY SALLY HOPKINSON, NEWLY APPOINTED PR GURU TO MR STEVEN SPEEDBERG, ON HER RETURN FROM THE BIG SMOKE:

1. They are taking offices just over the road from her old firm, X Communications. It just so happens that these offices are twice as big and three times as nice as her old offices, thank you very MUCH.

2. Mum is head of cons* for Mr Speedberg's next blockbuster, which will be announced soon – and you'll never guess what it's going to be called⸮ YES – *Black Beauty*. But that is TOP SECRET. (History will note that I had that information first and never told anyone.)

Mum met Charmian Chichester at the railway station on her way back from London, and I think the conversation went something like this:

3. 'Well, you look very smart, Sally . . . What have YOU been up to . . .⸮ I must come over tomorrow and sort out my lease for the boutique outlet . . . By the way, there could be some work for you . . . We'll need some help in the shop sweeping up and stuff . . . I'm sure Daffodil would like to come and play . . .'

* CONS – making sure everyone believes your message even if it isn't true.

4. 'Oh, Charmian . . . That's so kind . . . I'm afraid I'm going to be a bit busy . . . In fact, I'm full-time in London these days with Steven Speedberg . . . Oh . . . didn't you hear . . .¿ Yes, he's going to be filming a blockbuster, and I'M IN CHARGE . . . and Holly's going to be quite busy too, so she might not have a lot of time to see Daffodil . . .'

I am going to have to teach Mum to 'stay on message'. Because Daffodil is OFFICIALLY my best friend again after I let her into my pub quiz team – even though she was rubbish at it – so I don't need Mum shaking that barrel of apples up and spilling the
milk
all over the place.

CHAPTER 37

WHO IS BADGER?

'SO WHAT DO WE KNOW ABOUT BADGER?' I ASKED MYSELF WITH MY BAND MANAGER'S SOCKS ON.

She turns up for an audition in the middle of nowhere sounding like the chocolate in the box that everyone wants to eat, infiltrates herself into the band and then upsets Harmony DOUBLE-WHOPPER big time.

So I'm asking myself some forenzied* questions to make sure I'm spit-spot and stuff.

* FORENZIED
– agitated and
criminological**.

** CRIMINOLOGICAL
– not quite sure what
it means, but it's a
terrifically long word.

1. Why did she want to be in the band in the first place? I don't want to blow smoke up Harold's nose, but he has got some way to go before he's knocking out Golden Oldies at the Albert Hall, if you get my drift. So why did she choose The Cool?

2. Why did she encourage Stickly to get all BOGGLE-EYED when they were hanging around in the trees? Is she an act of sabotage?

3. So is Badger actually a member of another band, and she's been sent in to cause ructions in The Cool?

4. Did I DOUBLE-WHOPPER knock it on the head first time round when I suspected that she might be a police insider snitching on the Hopkinson family?

5. Is this revenge by Union Jack Porker's Happy English Pork Pies at Happy Farm?

6. Did the police tip off Union Jack Porker's Happy English Pork Pies at Happy Farm?

Anyway, I still hadn't got a clue what she was flipping well up to when Harold caught me on the jump by confirming the **OFFICIAL** band practice.

This meant Badger would be coming and Harmony would be in the proximity of dangerous farmyard objects such as hammers, screwdrivers, saws, pliers and drills. And you don't have to be  a literary buffoon to know that history is littered with gruesome murders carried out with objects such as that, pardon my French.

Don't forget Harmony is a VERY passionate young lady with hormones and loads of blood flowing through her veins.

CHAPTER 38

INTERCEPTING BADGER

SO IT WAS DOUBLE-WHOPPER SPIT-SPOT TIME FOR MY MAGIC POCKET WATCH TO UNEARTH WHO BADGER REALLY IS BEFORE HARMONY TURNS GRANDPA'S FARMYARD INTO ONE OF THOSE MURDER SCENES ON *CRIMEWATCH*.

I skulked around in the farmyard pretending to collect eggs and clearing up some doings, so that I could see Badger off at the pass, as they say in cowboy films.

She was the first to arrive for the OFFICIAL start of band practice – and when I got a quick forenzied glance at the driver who dropped her off, I couldn't help but think that I'd seen her before.

'Hi, Badger,' I said, looking cool as a cucumber. 'Smart chauffeur.'

'Just my mum,' she replied in a sultry singer's tone.

'Oh . . . Well, would you mind coming into the chicken shed for a minute . . .? Just need to chat about band business . . .'

'Can't we go into the recording studio?'

'Er . . . no . . . It's booked for the next ten minutes.'

'Really?'

'Yes . . . really . . . We can just go in here . . . Don't worry about the pong . . . It's only chickens' doings.'

So I led Badger into the chicken shed and fished out my **MAGIC POCKET WATCH**.

'Look at my **MAGIC POCKET WATCH**, Badger.'

'Yes . . . It's very nice, Holly . . . Now what was it you wanted to talk about . . .?'

'Look . . . It goes backwards and forwards, forwards and backwards.'

And then I gave her three verses.

'SPIRO, SPERO, SQUIGGLEOUS SCOTCH,
CAST YOUR EYES WHITHER MY WATCH.'

Badger didn't put up any resistance to the hypnotic powers of my **MAGIC POCKET WATCH**.

'So, Badger . . . I have a few questions to ask you . . . and you will tell me the whole truth . . .'

'Yes, Holly.'

'Good . . . so are you working for the police?'

'What on earth makes you think that?'

'Yes or no, please,' I said sternly.

'No.'

'Right . . . Well, are you anything to do with another band?'

'NO . . . WHY WOULD I BE?'

'Hmmm . . . So what were you doing getting Stickly all BOGGLE-EYED when you were all up those trees?'

'Er . . . Well, I was trying to make Harold jealous.'

'WHAAAT . . .? WHY WERE YOU DOING THAT, FOR GOODNESS' SAKE?'

'Because I wanted Harold to be BOGGLE-EYED about ME!'

'So you upset Harmony to get at Harold . . . Is that what you're saying?'

'YES,' she replied, sticking her chin out like a meerkat and standing like a duck.

The time had come to be truthless without the 't'. If you don't manage these pop groups with a hot iron, they can get out of hand very quickly.

'Well, Badger . . . this is the thing . . . You are going to resign from the band . . . right now . . . VAMOOSE . . . So you'd better ring your mum PROMPTO and leave before the rest of the band turn up . . . And you will forget that we had this conversation . . . So it's ADIOS, MON AMI, as they say in Austria . . . and no hard feelings.'

'Yes, Holly,' she said, looking a bit shocked.

But shocked wasn't the word for Holly Hopkinson of Holly Hopkinson Band Manager Inc. when her mum drove back into the farmyard – you could have DOUBLE-WHOPPER knocked me over with ten tons of Turnip Scallopini with Pomegranate Seeds à la Plancha.

So guess who her mother flipping well is?

YES.

'The lady who brushes' – or should I say the lady who used to brush or even the lady who brushed?

Holly Hopkinson has just foiled a plot to destabilise the entire Hopkinson family – from Grandpa down to Harmony.

CHAPTER 39

MUM BACK AT WORK

BREAKING NEWS –

MUM CALLED DAD FROM HER NEW SWANKY OFFICES TODAY – AND SHE HAS GIVEN HIM **STRICT OFFICIAL** INSTRUCTIONS TO BUY A FOOD VAN.

'CAN YOU BELIEVE IT?'

he asked me in his 'hysterical chef' voice as he danced around the kitchen frightening the living daylights out of Barkley. 'I've got the job to do all the catering for a blockbuster.'

'Well, fancy that,' I said. 'So, Dad, can I just show you my **MAGIC POCKET WATCH** . . .? It's very lovely.'

'Can it wait, Holly . . .? I've got to get on to Catering-Vans-Are-Us.com.'

Sometimes parents just don't listen. But in the end Dad always does what I want him to do if I put on my cute face.

'Sorry, Holly . . . of course . . . What a lovely watch.'

So I only gave him two verses of **SPIRO, SPERO** because he's always putty in my hands.

'Dad . . . you are going to stop being a celebrity chef . . . It was my idea . . . I know . . . but it was a bad idea . . . so NO MORE!'

'Yes, Holly.'

'And no more exotic dishes in the Chequers . . . I know . . . also my idea . . . Back to very simple food for good honest folk . . . OK?'

'Yes, Holly.'

'And, while I'm at it, NO Vera in the blockbuster food van . . . DEFO-NIGHTLY.'

'Yes, Holly.'

I mean, can you imagine the carnage if Vera started feeding the blockbuster lot their lunch? After one of her **ROADKILL PIES** – and I know that's where she gets her meat from because I found a bit of number plate in my slice the other day – it would look like a battle scene in *The Lord of the Rings*, not *Black Beauty* (top secret). There would be a terrible queue for the bogs.

o o o

Once I'd sorted Dad out it was time to visit Le Prince and Declan with Grandpa.

Naturally I assumed that all would be fine and dandy at the stables now that the anti- and anti-anti housing weird people have all gone back to their homes (some irony there, thank you very much), but life is not a bed of roses on a nice heap of manure, as I am finding out.

Vinnie says that Le Prince is not one hundred per cent up for being covered in black dye and pretending to be Black Beauty. He says that he is a racehorse, not a show pony.

'Does he indeed . . .¿ Well, we shall see about that . . . Just give me five minutes alone with him,' I requested.

So I got my **MAGIC POCKET WATCH** out and marched right into Le Prince's stable and shut the door firmly behind me.

I gave him six verses of Spiro, Spero, which I think was one too many. He was so **GOGGLE-EYED** at one point that I thought they were going to pop right out.

'Le Prince . . . you are going to be Black Beauty . . . and be dyed . . . and do exactly what Mr Speedberg asks you to do . . . then you can have extra rations of oats and go back to being a racehorse . . . Happy with that¿'

Le Prince gave what could have been a nod, so I think it worked.

One glimmer of a lightning bolt at the end of the rainbow is that Declan has ventured out of his stable – encouraged by CHICKEN who is coming good on the mentoring front – and was able to stretch his legs without freaking out. Hardly the sort of performance that will win the Chequers Xmas Pony Race, but it's four legs in the right direction.

Now for the **BAD NEWS** – well, bad news for Harold anyway. He was playing up all over the place when Grandpa and I got back to the farmyard.

'It's a **DISASTER** . . . Badger's quit the band . . . She's just walked out without telling us why.'

'No way?' I said, all innocently. 'That's very odd . . . How's Stickly taken the news?'

'Oh . . . He doesn't seem too bothered . . . He says singers are ten a penny . . . We'll have to start auditioning again.'

Then Harmony came mooching along like song-writers do.

'Terrible news about Badger,' I said, practically scraping myself off the floor.

'Like . . . good riddance . . . She was SOOO overrated . . . Anyway I'm, like, writing a tragic song about the band breaking up . . . It's like my inspiration.'

'EXCELLENTO,'

I said in my Icelandic voice.

CHAPTER 40

THIS IS WHY MUM IS A GURU

SO I HAPPENED TO BE LOOKING THROUGH THE PAPERS IN MUM'S BAG THIS MORNING. NO, NOT BEING NOSY, JUST SEEING IF THERE WAS ANYTHING I COULD HELP OUT WITH. THANK YOU VERY MUCH.

And I discovered why she is a guru. Even though she has landed

THE BIGGEST

PR JOB IN THE WORLD,

SHE HAS NOT DROPPED THE DUMMY

AS FAR AS VILLAGE AFFAIRS ARE

CONCERNED – OH NO.

BELOW IS ROUGHLY WHAT SHE HAS SKETCHED OUT ON A PIECE OF PAPER.

✖ STEP 1 – Mum is going to get the vicar to reschedule the Yuletide Log Competition and hold it in the village hall at the same time as the village children's and dogs' fancy dress show.

✖ STEP 2 – Mum is going to get Aunt Electra to cancel the Chequers Festive Fancy Dress Party for Cats and Children – that is in exchange for getting the Chequers the gig of doing the food van for the blockbuster film.

✖ STEP 3 – In exchange for Mrs Smartside not protesting about the ten Olde Worlde houses, Mum is telling her that Aunt Electra will cancel her Festive Fancy Dress Party for Cats and Children, AND Mum is going to invite Mrs Smartside to play bridge with Mr Speedberg.

✖ STEP 4 – Mum is telling Vince that his Yuletide Log Competition is back on as long as he doesn't mind Dad's food van parked up on his farm.

Then Mum added at the bottom of her sketch:

POTENTIAL PROBLEM –
nothing in this for
Charmian Chichester!!

Mum seems to be rather good at getting other people to do what she wants them to do, even if it's not really in their best interests – maybe that's what PR is?

CHAPTER 41

DAD'S NEW MENU

SO DAD MADE HIS **OFFICIAL**
ANNOUNCEMENT TODAY TO VERA AND
AUNT ELECTRA THAT THE CHEQUERS IS
GOING 'RAW IS MORE' WITH ITS MENU.

SOMETHING'S GONE WRONG HERE.

All the food served in the Chequers will be sourced from Grandpa's farm. That is obviously, long-term, not great news for the sheep, pigs and cows that go round doing their doings all over the place. And it will be quite demanding of Florence if Dad goes for a lot of yoghurt menus. She'll be pumping the stuff out 24/7.

To start with, Dad was flatulenced* (again) by Mrs Beeton.

And where better to start than raw beef sandwiches – which is not just chopping an animal up and slapping it between two bits of bread, thank you very much. Oh no – the meat has to be rubbed through a wire sieve and then spread on to 'dainty squares' of bread.

HE HAS BEEN READING about fancy restaurants in the south of France and he's going to pull a great stunt that they all do down there.

What they do is sell a big basket of raw vegetables and give the customers a bowl of dip, which is WAY TOO SMALL to stick all the veg in the basket into.

So GUESS WHAT?

* FLATULENCED – what will happen to anyone who eats this stuff.

SIMPLES.

They can't eat all the veg when the dip runs dry, so the rest goes back into the kitchen and they just sell it again. Dad thinks he can sell a giant tomato about three times every lunch.

The first **BIG MENU NEWS**, however, is that Dad is going to do an all-pheasant menu because it's December and not much else is growing.

I told him that the local country folk wouldn't be very happy about that and he said, 'Pheasant, not peasant, Holly.'

☆ **SOUP COURSE –**
Pheasant and Bramble Broth

☆ **FIRST COURSE –** Pheasant Sashimi

☆ **MAIN COURSE –** Chilled Raw
Pheasant Stew with Boiled Potatoes
and Hedgerow Ratatouille

☆ **PUDDING –** Pheasant Rarebit
(with a bit of Florence's cheese mixed in)

The pheasant sashimi will be his USP* selling point – his signature dish – so I think that's going to be

BIG NEWS.

USP* – Undisputed Superb Product. Dad is almost guaranteeing that no roadkill products will be in any of his dishes.

CHAPTER 42

DECLAN TRAINING SESSION

THERE ARE TIMES WHEN YOU JUST
HAVE TO **THROW YOURSELF**
INTO THE POOL OFF THE DIVING BOARD
AND REMEMBER TO KEEP YOUR MOUTH
CLOSED AND YOUR NOSE SHUT.

The Chequers Xmas Pony Race is only a couple of days away, so if Declan and I are going to nail those other kids and win the best food prize, we have got to spit-spot.

So Grandpa and I went up to Vince's farm ready for me to do a bit of jockey action.

'Vinnie, it's moose or man time for Holly Hopkinson. Please prepare Declan for a full rehearsal . . . which will be . . . left-handed circles . . . flat out in a straight line . . . emergency braking . . . a bit of bending-race stuff and then standing still by a bucket in case Aunt Electra throws her BOHEMIAN apple-bobbing thing in.'

'Riight,' Vinnie said while pulling unhelpful faces. 'But—'

'Excuse you, Vinnie . . . There are no buts in the world of Holly Hopkinson Film Location and Places Inc. Declan's only knee-high to a grasshopper . . . How hard can it be?'

'Thing is—'

'No more pulling faces, please, Vinnie . . . This is how we roll.'

Grandpa was making wheezing noises like an amused car tyre that has driven over a bucket of rusty nails. He seems to think the prospect of me riding Declan is highly amusing.

When Vinnie brought Declan out, he was shaking like Slinky Dave's bus does when it goes down the lane to Grandpa's farm.

'What's the matter with him now?' I asked.

''E's cold,' advised Vinnie.

'Well, we'll soon warm him up.'

So I got Vinnie to leg me up on Declan and we set off into the field at a brisk trot. And everything went fine to start with.

It was when I tried to turn right that I realised Declan's steering wheel doesn't work – so I tried to turn left and it didn't work that way either. So we just kept going straight on – quite fast to start with, and then faster, then really very fast straight out of the field and into Mrs Smartside's orchard; some doofus had left the gate open.

AND GUESS
WHAT HAPPENED NEXT?

I ended up with Mrs Smartside's flipping washing line wrapped round my neck, and I got swaddled like an EGYPTIAN MUMMY in Mrs Smartside's underwear, pardon my French.

Luckily there was no sign of her, so Declan and I spit-spot as quick as we could, leaving behind a TERRIBLE MESS.

"E needs another 'oss to folla,' Vinnie advised after Declan and I had retraced our footsteps. "E's only a baby.'

'Hmmm . . . well, what about Le Prince . . .? You could ride him, Vinnie.'

But Vinnie just shook his head. It turned out Le Prince was covered from head to toe in some very strong black dye that hadn't dried, and he was not too happy about that either.

BEST FRIEND NEWS – just when all seemed to be without hope, GUESS WHO came trotting past Vince's farm on her pony?

YES.

MY RECENTLY REAPPOINTED BEST FRIEND Daffodil Chichester.

'Hey, Holly . . . How's it going? I didn't know you'd taken up riding . . . Great . . . We can go for rides together.'

'Hey, Daffodil . . . Yes . . . that will be great . . . The thing is . . . it's not going too well . . . In fact . . . we've got a bit of a problem.'

This was a situation when Holly Hopkinson needed a best friend and Daffodil came through double-whopper big time with extra rations.

CHAPTER 43

DECLAN GETS BOGGLE EYES

IT TURNS OUT THAT DECLAN HAS TAKEN A BIT OF A SHINE TO POPPY – DAFFODIL'S PONY – AND IS NEEDING NO ENCOURAGEMENT TO FOLLOW HER WHEREVER SHE GOES. SO WE DID LEFT-HAND BENDS, RIGHT-HAND BENDS, STRAIGHT LINES, EMERGENCY STOPS AND BENDING PRACTICE.

As long as Poppy led the way, Declan was spit-spot double-quick time. But it did leave one problem unresolved – and that problem is:

HOW CAN I WIN THE CHEQUERS XMAS PONY RACE IF DECLAN HAS TO FOLLOW POPPY EVERYWHERE?

No one had told me that ponies get boggle-eyed – but that is what has happened to Declan.

CHAPTER 44

THE VILLAGE CHILDREN'S AND DOGS' FANCY DRESS SHOW

Or to give it its full title:

THE VILLAGE CHILDREN'S AND DOGS' FANCY DRESS SHOW IN ASSOCIATION WITH THE YULETIDE LOG COMPETITION AND THE CHEQUERS FESTIVE FANCY DRESS PARTY FOR CATS AND CHILDREN. (IF YOU HAVEN'T GOT A CAT, BRING A DOG.)

― MEDIA NEWS ―

Neither the *Daily Chipping Topley Mail* nor RoundaboutChippingTopley.com have given this event its full title, which has caused great offence.

Mum insists she gave the media a full PR briefing AND the full name so it's the fault of 'lazy journalists' that they called it 'LOWER GORING FANCY DOG SHOW'.

It all got off to a shaky start because the vicar – who is still turning up to OFFICIAL stuff in a fireman's helmet, THE LUNATIC – blessed everyone and said it was in the festive spirit that everyone had come together in harmony.

So he's got that wrong.

1. It has nothing to do with Harmony, who isn't coming to the show because she's in the middle of writing her TRAGIC song.

2. There wasn't much 'coming together in harmony' when Baby Jesus had to be born in a STABLE, thank you very much. There would be carnage, absolute carnage, if people carried on like that these days and turned away women who were about to have babies.

EMERGENCY COMMITTEE NEWS

– YOU WILL NOT BELIEVE THIS – when it was full-on war between the Chequers and the VCEOC Mrs Smartside and Mrs Chichester held an emergency secret meeting of the VCEOC and shut it down – behind Mum's back. Then they had another meeting and formed a new committee WITHOUT Mum or Vince or Vera. BUT they have failed to attract a celebrity to open the show – Mrs Chichester had made noises about some cushion designer who is so un-celebrity that I don't even know his name.

Of course Mum would have been in a VERY good position to supply a celebrity ribbon cutter. For **two reasons:**

1. She is married to one now, even if he's just retired.

2. She's working for one – but I think he'll be a bit busy for the dog show.

So when they came crawling to Mum with their fancy tails between their legs asking for help, Mum told Mrs Smartside and Mrs Chichester that she was too busy to be phoning around at the last minute.

Mum is no fool.

So guess who opened the fancy dog show?

YES.

Mrs Smartside – in the same hat that she had on to open the village fete.

And I heard with my red-herring hearing what Mrs Smartside said under her breath during the opening ceremony – so she should resign from the new committee unless she wants me to put the record straight in my memoirs. Or report her to the vicar.

YULETIDE LOG NEWS – the new committee have come to an agreement with Vince. All the logs will be placed anonymously in the kitchen part of the village hall so that they can be judged on their merits.

FANCY DOG ENTRIES NEWS – Mum entered me and Barkley without asking me, thank you very much. And Barkley rolled in some cows' doings just before we had to leave for the village hall without asking me, so the pong coming off him is really bad.

I am furious, **ABSOLUTELY FURIOUS**.

But, on the positive side, Vera has made him a nice festive Xmas bow to go round his neck. She tried to put one on me too but I told her to cut it out.

I'm not turning up to the village hall dressed up like a dog, thank you very much.

My best friend Daffodil Chichester, on the other hand, arrived looking like a decoration in her mother's shop.

WHAT DID SHE THINK

SHE LOOKED LIKE?

Of course, as she's my best friend, I was very supportive and told her she looked amazing – well, as amazing as a human Christmas tree can possibly look. There was something distinctly weird about her eyes appearing near where the fairy's feet should have been. And I've never heard of people hanging embroidered candles on their Christmas trees. Her black Labrador was not enjoying the holly wreath tied round its neck and was constantly trying to bite it, like it had fleas.

Next through the door came Felicity Snoop – and it WON'T surprise you to know that her black Labrador was dressed up as a reindeer.

´ YES. ´

Antlers and all. Obviously she went and stood next to Daffodil after making an unnecessary fuss about Barkley's pong and holding her nose as if it was about to fall off.

Then Amaryllis and Iris arrived, holding hands like they were two peas in a drum kit. And, just to make the point, their black Labrador puppies had exactly the same Xmas festive leads on.

Everyone went

'ahhh'

and made a TERRIFIC fuss of them.

That left poor little Crocus coming in on her own – and I can see what's happened now: Amaryllis and Iris have frozen Crocus out of their group.

So I said, 'Crocus, would you and your black Labrador like to come and stand next to me and Barkley?' And, bigger than that, I already had it in mind to invite her to join the Bogey Club.

AND DO YOU KNOW

WHAT SHE SAID?

'Poo-ee . . . What is that stink . . .? Is that you, Holly . . .? What did you have for lunch?'

'EXCUSE YOU,' I replied in my 'very offended' voice. 'You're not smelling so good yourself . . . thank you very much.'

So that's her invitation to join the Bogey Club gone west down the River Topley without a paddle or a life jacket in sight.

I'VE **NEVER** HEARD
ANYTHING LIKE IT.

Then, late as ever, the boys came crashing in – Wolfe, Gaspar and Tiger. They are like a pack of feral wolves – and their black Labradors were not much better behaved. There was tinsel flying everywhere and Gaspar had covered his in gold sparkle dust just to remind us that he's named after one of the wise men – as if we didn't know.

Then they started on Barkley's pong.

'Ugh . . . What's that stink . . .¿ Who's done one . . .¿ Call an ambulance . . . Call the fire brigade,' the boys shouted, thinking they were VERY FUNNY.

THIS IS OFFICIALLY

THE LAST TIME I TAKE BARKLEY

TO A DOG SHOW.

Then guess what happened next¿

Vinnie arrived.

But nobody had told him the Chequers Festive Fancy Dress Party for Cats and Children had OFFICIALLY been dropped for this new carry-on. So in Vinnie walks, bold as brass, dressed as Dick Whittington with our Moggy under his arm.

'All riight?' says Vinnie, completely unaware that he has got the dress code desperately **wrong**.

UNFORTUNATELY Moggy has better dress sense than Vinnie and decided to get out of that village hall as fast as her legs would carry her.

THANKFULLY Moggy is a gnat's whisker quicker than black Labradors when it comes to escaping from village halls.

But REALLY,

TERRIBLY,

UNFORTUNATELY,

as far as the entrants of the Yuletide Log Competition were concerned, Moggy made her (successful) escape right through the Yuletide logs.

I think history may have been made in Lower Goring today – because I can't think that there can ever have been a Yuletide Log Competition that got abandoned twice in the same year before.

CHAPTER 45

THE HOPKINSONS' FIRST GOLDEN AWARD

SO WE WERE ALL MOOCHING AROUND THE KITCHEN THIS MORNING DOING OUR THINGS:

- GRANDPA – noggin in the *Racing Post.*

- DAD – upside down in Mrs Beeton's cookbook.

- MUM – spit-spotting mushed avocado and chilli on to some toast before she tears out of the door to the railway station, barking instructions.

- VERA – muttering into an ironing basket full of Grandpa's pants.

- HARMONY – weeping into her songbook about the **TRAGIC** ballad that's she's writing.

✿ **HAROLD** – picking his nose and wondering.

✿ **HOLLY HOPKINSON** – trying to work out what's going to go wrong next.

And GUESS WHAT HAPPENED NEXT?

YES.

One of those TV vans with a big satellite dish on its roof came bouncing down the lane to the farmyard.

'Oh, for goodness' sake . . . I haven't got the right make-up on . . . Holly . . . can you tell them I'm not here?' Mum said in her 'PR' voice.

Since when did Holly Hopkinson of Holly Hopkinson Film Location and Places Inc. become my mother's flunky, THANK you **very** much?

But I know that keeping your bread buttered on both sides of the piece of toast is what you do in the film business, so I OBLIGED – on this occasion.

'She says she's not in,' I told the van driver in my 'polite' voice.

'Who says she's not in?' he replied.

'MY MOTHER, OF COURSE . . .
EXCUSE YOU.'

'But we've come to do an interview with George Hopkinson.'

'Well, you can cut that out – he isn't a celebrity chef any more.'

'But he's won an award . . . and we need to interview him,' the van driver insisted.

Then it dawned on me that I might be missing something here.

'Pray, what award, monsieur?' I asked in a 'Spanish' accent to throw him off the track that I might have been barking up the wrong bush.

'Haven't you heard . . .? It's all over the NEWS . . . He's won the Gamekeepers Simple Recipe of the Year GOLDEN COUNTRYSIDE Award.'

'No way . . . You're kidding me . . . You aren't from that acting school that Aunt Electra keeps getting people from are you?'

And then I remembered that she hadn't ACTUALLY hired a Steven Speedberg lookalike after all.

'No, miss . . . We're from a national television station . . . Can we please speak to George Hopkinson?'

And that is how we found out that Dad has become a SERIOUS world-famous cooker of food.

 THE HOPKINSON FAMILY

 ARE ON A BIG ROLL, BABY . . .

as they say in Hollywood.

CHAPTER 46

CHEQUERS XMAS PONY RACE – THE BUILD-UP

SO TODAY IS THE DAY HOLLY HOPKINSON IS GOING TO PUT HER NECK ON THE LINE DEFENDING THE HONOUR OF THE HOPKINSON FAMILY. EVEN THOUGH DECLAN AND I ARE FAR FROM MATCH FIT.

So if this is where my memoirs end, I hope posterity will remember me fondly.

I thought about texting Aleeshaa and asking her to come down – but today I need Daffodil Chichester to be my best friend, not Aleeshaa.

Some of the feral kids in the pony race are nutters. So I AM VERY, COMPLETELY,

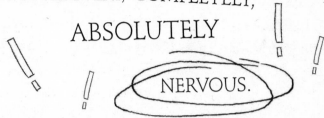

ABSOLUTELY

NERVOUS.

But I can't let anyone know that – particularly Declan and Vinnie, who I visited at the crack of dawn.

'How is Declan today?' I asked Vinnie without fear or trepidation in my voice – much.

'BOGGLE-EYED 'e is,' Vinnie replied.

'I don't mean that department, Vinnie . . . Is he ready to run like the wind round the church . . . and then do a bit of bending . . . and some cow-poo apple bobbing if need be?' (Florence has tipped me off about that bit.)

''E'll follow Poppy anywhere.'

'Well, I suppose that's a start . . . as long as Daffodil and Poppy don't hang about smelling candles and cushions all day . . . I need to have a word with my BEST FRIEND.'

Everyone at the farm was being far too helpful and annoying. Even Vera, who asked me what I'd like for breakfast. But I wasn't that desperate. You'd have thought I was off to the gallows.

So I decided to spit-spot down to the Chequers to check out the prizes – and they are NOT BAD.

⭐ **WINNING JOCKEY** – barrel of beer. (If we win that, I'll give it to Harold because pop stars all drink a lot of beer.)

⭐ **WINNING PONY** – sack of carrots. (Declan likes apples, not carrots. So if we win that, I'll give the carrots to Vera for her Christmas present.)

⭐ **OWNER OF WINNING PONY** – bag of meat from Sir Garfield, Dad's butcher friend, but there's a note saying he can't guarantee the Provence* of the meat – so it's probably not from France.

As Grandpa owns Declan that will be his prize if we're triumphant – so he can give it to Vera for Christmas too.

> * PROVENCE –
> area of France
> sometimes
> confused with
> origin or source.

That will save her a bit of shopping.

I found Daffodil in the Chequers car park pampering Poppy and making her look all shiny.

'What are you doing, Daffodil?' I asked in my 'jockey' voice.

'Just making her look nice,' Daffodil replied.

'Daffodil . . . this is a race.'

'Well, Poppy and I are just going to go nice and quietly at the back,' Daffodil affirmed.

ON NO YOU'RE NOT, I NEARLY REPLIED –

BUT INSTEAD I PULLED OUT

my MAGIC POCKET WATCH.

'Daffodil . . . have I ever shown you my MAGIC POCKET WATCH . . . ? Just look very carefully at it . . . backwards and forwards . . . forwards and backwards.'

And I gave her three verses of **SPIRO, SPERO** – nice and slowly.

'Daffodil,' I said in my 'official best friend' voice, 'you are going to go like the clappers when the race starts . . . Don't worry about falling off or anything like that . . . Just go for it . . . **COMPRENDO?**'

Daffodil gave a satisfactory nod.

'That's the spirit, Daffodil . . . The Charge of the Light Brigade . . . See you at the starting line, MON BRAVE* . . . And, Daffodil . . . thank you . . . I love having you as my **BEST FRIEND**.'

Massive crowds, including all of Mum's computers, were gathering in front of the pub – in fact, it was getting out of hand even before three coachloads of gamekeepers arrived to try the Raw is More pheasant set menu.

Aunt Electra was in her ELEMENT. 'Oh . . . it's like the Palio in Siena . . . So much passion and energy in the air . . . All these brave gladiators going out to do battle.'

* MON BRAVE – what the French say when they're terrified.

'Excuse you, Aunt Electra . . . but can you cut it out . . . ؟ I'm flipping well nervous enough, thank you VERY much,' I informed my aunt, who is the only person I can admit to being nervous to.

'Oh, good luck, Holly . . . I'm SO proud of you . . . Just do your best . . . That's all you can do,' Aunt Electra said in her 'passionate' voice, and then she gave me one of her wet smackers on the cheek.

DISGUSTING.

The vicar had been given the job of telling everyone what the rules were, so he stood on the graveyard wall in his full shepherd's outfit – crook and washing-up cloth wrapped round his head. 'Gather round, my flock,' he shouted.

Oh, **very clever** – so that's what the stupid outfit's all about.

'Children . . . jockeys . . . combatants . . . let's have a nice clean race . . . No foul play . . . When I blow my shepherd's horn, the race will start . . . Round the church . . . back up the cricket pitch . . . through Gerald's bending poles . . . and then dismount to get ONE apple out of the Chequers mystery barrel . . . Feed the apple to your pony AFTER you've rinsed it . . . and then back on your pony to the finishing line by the Chequers.'

'What's in the barrel?' shouted either Wolfe or Tiger.

'That's a surprise, children . . . but don't eat it or drink it. And now it gives me great pleasure to announce that Mr Steven Spe . . . berg will be starting the race . . . and Mrs Sm—'

The computers and the gamekeepers all went wild when they heard Mr Speedberg's name mentioned, so no one heard that Mrs Smartside was going to be the judge. Apparently she is MASSIVE in the finishing-line-judge world.

Then the ponies started gathering in the car park. Felicity Snoop was obviously bang on time and looking all professional; Gaspar, Wolfe and Tiger sort of looked the part, whereas Iris, Crocus and Amaryllis looked like they were off to the ballet.

It wasn't that lot I was worried about. It was the 'Vinnie cousins lookalikes' that were **FRIGHTENING** me; they have a hungry look in their eyes, and so do their wiry ponies, even if they are a bit old.

But there was ABSOLUTELY no sign of Vinnie and Declan.

'Where are they, for flip's sake?' I asked Grandpa and Vince.

'They're on their way . . . Don't panic,' Grandpa said, putting his hand on my shoulder and patting it gently. He's never done that before.

'Ah,' grunted Vince.

And then guess who came round the corner holding hands with treble-whopper **BOGGLE EYES?**

YES.

287

Harmony and Stickly.

'GOOD LUCK, HOLLY ...
WE **LOVE** YOU.'

Not the sort of distraction I needed right now, thank you very much.

Then Mum and Dad popped up. 'Good luck, darling . . . Be careful . . . Don't be too brave . . . Hold on tight,' they chortled.

Even goofy Harold had turned up, on the right day for once. 'Go steady, little sis,' he called. 'Events, dear boy, events.'

'Cut it out, Harold,' I replied.

FINALLY Vinnie and Declan deigned to put an appearance in, just when I thought I was going to be doing the flipping race on my own trotters.

'Where the heck have you been?' I asked Vinnie.

'Keeping 'im quiet round the corner with Chicken.'

'Oh . . . Well, how is Declan today?'

'All riight.'

'EXCELLENTO . . . Well, we'll just have a quick chat . . . if that's OK with you, Vinnie . . . and we'll be right over.'

So I took Declan into a quiet corner and got my **MAGIC POCKET WATCH** out.

Three verses seemed to do the trick.

'Declan . . . you are going to do anything and everything you can to win this flipping race . . . by foul means or fair, Declan . . . I DO NOT want any sense of fair play that you may have to get in the way . . . *COMPRENDO . . .?* This is your ticket to a quiet life, Declan.'

I think Declan nodded.

'WELL, FULL STEAM AHEADO,'

I said out of the corner of my mouth like horse people do.

CHAPTER 47

THE START

'IT'S A GREAT HONOUR TO BE
INVOLVED IN AN INSTITUTION THAT GOES
BACK CENTURIES,' MR SPEEDBERG DRAWLED
IN HIS COWBOY HAT, STANDING ON TOP OF
THE STRAW BALES FROM WHICH HE WAS
GOING TO START THE CHEQUERS XMAS
PONY RACE IN RELATIVE SAFETY.

'Where the heck DOES he think he is?' I asked
Daffodil, who knows absolutely everything about
history.

'The Colosseum in Rome?' Daffodil suggested.

This is the FIRST time Aunt Electra's done this
race . . . It has NO history,' I pointed out.

'Maybe Boudicca had some races here?' Daffodil replied.

'Excuse you, Daffodil . . . I don't think so . . . She didn't have time for a get-together before Christmas to see who could get back to the pub first . . . That's the trouble with Hollywoodians . . . You give them a simple bit of history and they scramble it.'

Anyway, all Daffodil's chat meant that we were NOT right in the front as the ponies lined up. But guess who was when Mr Speedberg shouted 'AND THEY'RE OFF'?

- YES. -

Felicity Snoop got a flying start, of course, followed by the pack of feral kids and the posh boys (Wolfe, Tiger and Gaspar).

Daffodil and I were only just in front of the flowers (Iris, Crocus and Amaryllis).

'Be careful, Daffodil, darling,' Mrs Chichester shouted unhelpfully.

'Be reckless,' I shouted louder, 'and flipping well get Poppy to spit-spot.'

Then, to my amazement, Declan sank his teeth into Poppy's bottom and she took off like a nuclear missile.

The next bit is a blur. All I KNOW is that no one has ever approached a graveyard at such speed in their lives – not that graveyards are places that people rush to – and I have never heard such a din in all my life. Daffodil was screeching her head off as Poppy went flat out past the posh boys.

Thankfully Poppy turned left and followed Felicity Snoop and the feral kids, so we were in quite a nifty position by the time we got to the far end of the graveyard.

Given that Declan has no steering wheel, all I could do was to hang on for grim life. If Poppy didn't make the bend, Declan and I would be in the River Topley.

Luckily Poppy is not that intrepid, and she was not going to leave the herd to escape from Declan's gnashers.

By the time we got to Sir Garfield's bending poles, the feral kids were in front and Poppy was neck and neck with Felicity Snoop. The feral kids were spit-spot through the bending poles – they're probably used to that sort of stuff – but a couple of them were going so fast they overshot the apple-bob barrel.

The gamekeepers were making one heck of a noise, shouting their heads off and whistling like their dogs had run off. But if the crowd thought it was all over,

THEY WERE VERY
MUCH MISTAKEN.

Felicity Snoop got to the apple bobbing just after the most controlled feral kid, followed by Poppy/Daffodil and then me/Declan – who obediently pulled up right next to the barrel.

Aunt Electra had been very careful to keep what the apples were bobbing in a secret – apart from the warning that it should not be consumed in any way – and that hands were allowed.

There were good reasons for that – because it was liquid COW POO – no joking.

As soon as the semi-feral kid's pony smelled it, it took off over the horizon – never to be seen again.

Daffodil took one whiff of the barrel and was immediately sick – luckily not into the apple bobbing, or that really would have been the end of that, thank you very much.

Felicity Snoop is so clever by half that she hadn't listened to the instructions – and instead of using her hand, she put her head into the barrel. And that did NOT play out well for her. It will be some time before Felicity Snoop is ready for action again.

I just held my nose and fished an apple out with my hand – quite frankly it wasn't much different from collecting eggs in Grandpa's farmyard.

I had the apple rinsed off in a jiffy and Declan munched it down in double-quick time.

All I had to do was hop back on to Declan – which is no more challenging than hopping on to a sausage dog – and tear through Mrs Smartside's finishing tape.

CHAPTER 48

CELEBRATIONS

I'VE SEEN SOME **WILD** STUFF IN MY TIME – BUT NOTHING HAD PREPARED ME FOR THE **MAYHEM** THAT KICKED OFF.

Mrs Smartside clapped very loudly and cheered, 'Well done, Holly.'

Declan was exhausted and had to sit down while Vinnie went totally mad and threw loads of shapes and did stuff like a **LUNATIC**.

Harmony collapsed into Stickly's arms, weeping and saying it was the happiest day of her life – which seemed to be fine with Stickly.

Harold was singing 'She is the champion' from the tree he'd climbed up into – and Sir Speedberg came and five-at-fived me like I was a cowboy, shouting, 'You're the girl.'

I thought it might be a good moment to discuss my contract with him, but I got swept up into Mum and Dad's arms.

'Holly . . . you were amazing,' they were shouting as they kissed me all over the place. Which was jolly nice but it is rather embarrassing when your parents get emotional – so I tried to calm them down.

Grandpa was laughing his head off with Sir Garfield, who just shouted, 'Get that barrel open.' I assume he was referring to the beer, not the apple bobbing.

Aunt Electra was flying all over the place and talking in lots of different languages except English.

'Mio fantini, mio fantini,' she kept yelling.

I think she may have got caught up in Mr Speedberg's history nonsense.

And guess who actually had a smile on her face, from her nose to her chin, and was going to the beer barrel with Grandpa?

YES.

Vera. And she actually looked happy.

'Well done, my lamb,' the vicar said as he gave me a pat on my head.

I hope he doesn't keep this shepherd thing up all Christmas or it will drive us up the wall.

Then Daffodil came and gave me a hug. 'Well done, Holly,' she said. 'You were very brave . . . I hope we'll always be best friends.'

'Can we be if I never ride a pony ever again in my life?' I asked. 'Because I think I'm done with ponies now.'

'WE CAN BE BEST FRIENDS WHATEVER YOU DO,'

said Daffodil.

CHAPTER 49

GRAND PRIZEGIVING

THERE WAS A BIT OF AN ARGY-BARGY AROUND THE GRAND PRIZEGIVING STRAW BALES.

Even the bloke from the *Daily Chipping Topley Mail* and the woman from the Roundabout Chipping-Topley.com website started jostling each other for position.

Mrs Smartside (usual hat) assumed that because she'd done the finishing-line tape, she would be presenting a prize. But Aunt Electra was getting her sharp elbows into the mix; after all, the GENIUS of this pony race was entirely hers.

Mum told Aunt Electra that Dad was officially the chef (ex-celebrity) of the Chequers, so he should be up on the straw bales with her and Mr Speedberg.

BUT THEN THE BIGGEST SURPRISE OF ALL HAPPENED. AND IT TURNED THE GRAND PRIZEGIVING CEREMONY

into one of the biggest events Lower Goring has EVER seen.

So guess who popped up from nowhere looking like he was on his way to a VERY GOOD party?

YES.

The famous shepherd and singer Ed Shear'um.

'Hey, it's the Lower Goring rockers*,' Ed roared as he 'galloped into town' on his white stallion**.

* LOWER GORING ROCKERS – Volume I readers will already know Ed turned up to our *School of Rock* performance.

** STALLION – he was really in an electric car and he was looking for somewhere to charge it up because his flipping battery had nearly run out.

Anyway, **DOUBLE-WHOPPER** treble-quick-time,
Ed jumped up on the straw bales and bellowed,

'I DECLARE HOLLY HOPKINSON
THE WINNER.'

In my speech I desiccated*** my victory to
Vinnie and Declan. Not that Declan cared. He had
just about recovered enough to find Poppy and do
some **BOGGLE-EYED** stuff in the car park.

*** DESICCATED –
dedicating something
to someone without
blubbing.

CHAPTER 50

GRAND CELEBRATION

ALTHOUGH IT'S QUITE EMBARRASSING WHEN MY FAMILY DO THEIR EMOTIONAL GO-WEIRD STUFF, I HAVE TO ADMIT THAT TODAY WAS A VERY HAPPY DAY FOR HOLLY HOPKINSON OF HOLLY HOPKINSON FILM LOCATION AND PLACES INC.

BUT OBVIOUSLY IT WOULDN'T BE COOL TO ADMIT THAT TO ANYONE – NOT EVEN AUNT ELECTRA.

What I really loved is that everyone joined in.

Vera was tickled pink with her early Christmas present and she's going to make a giant carrot cake.

Vinnie brought Le Prince, looking all MAGNIFICENT and **BLACK**, down to the Chequers with Chicken to celebrate with Declan.

Harmony has started writing a song about a depraved kid* from the back streets of London who wins the biggest horse race in the world.

Harold and Stickly keep carrying me around the Chequers on their shoulders, shouting 'Events, dear boy, events' like DOOFUSES.

And Dad is back on top of the world.

The Hopkinson family live to fight another volume.

* DEPRAVED KID
– righteous kid who doesn't have any ponies.

EPILOGUE

WELL, THAT JUST ABOUT WRAPS UP
VOLUME II OF MY MEMOIRS – ALTHOUGH I
DO HAVE SOME **GOOD NEWS** TO REPORT,
THANK YOU VERY MUCH.

The driver arrived from the Amazon today with my iPad.

'This place is very difficult to find,' he said.

'Well, I suppose it is,' I said. 'So I guess from your base you drove up to Bogotá . . . the capital of Columbia, of course . . . Then on to Caracas in Venezuela . . . where I'll bet you picked up a load of those music shakers . . . On to the ferry to Southampton and then a nice run-up to Chipping Topley . . . but it IS a bit tricky from there.'

'Been round Chipping Topley all over the place . . . then found the Chequers in Lower Goring . . . The woman there . . . she is strange.'

'Excuse you . . . That would be Aunt Electra . . .'

'Can you sign here, please . . .?'

'ADIOS,'

I said nice and loudly in my 'Brazilian' voice. 'And I hope the ferry journey isn't too bad on the way home.'

So the business empire of Holly Hopkinson is now set to implode on to the world stage as soon as I get this iPad charged up.

And you can take it from me – even though we have been banished to an open-plan animal bog near Lower Goring – the Hopkinson family are going places.

As far as my **MAGIC POCKET WATCH** is concerned, I still haven't really worked out when it won't work.

But that is AU REVOIR AND OUT, as they say in the army cricket team.

SOME BANGING STARTED UPSTAIRS IN THE LOFT.

Quite loud to start with, and then even louder – and then very loud.

I was about to shout, 'Stop being annoying, Harold!' but then I realised he was sitting on my bed.

So it must flipping well be Mabel.

But she doesn't exist – or does she?

DISCOVER WHERE HOLLY'S
FIASCOS ALL BEGAN . . .

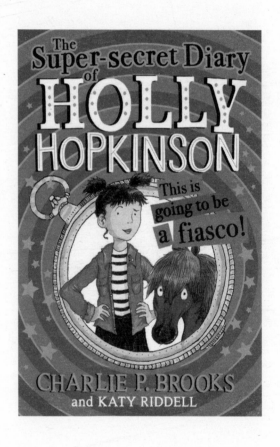

THIS IS ME

PROLOGUE

THESE ARE THE *LIVE* MEMOIRS OF HOLLY HOPKINSON, WHO IS NEARLY TEN.

I am writing them by my own fair hand so that historians and people from all over the world will have a real-life account of what life was like in twenty-first-century London without all the usual rubbish that adults put in.

Who knows how far in the future it will be before *you* get to read them, dear reader. I imagine it could be hundreds – even squillions – of years before they are dug up,

☆ published to international bestselling acclaim,

☆ set behind glass at the British Museum,

☆ studied in schools across the country

and

☆ turned into a Hollywood movie . . .

★ THE SUPER
SECRET DIARY
OF
HOLLY HOPKINSON:
THE MOVIE ★

If Hollywood still exists!

My family, THE HOPKINSONS, live in a lovely, warm, clean, modern house, thank you very much. My dad has a job in an office. I have *no* idea what he does, but he always wears a suit.

Mum works in PR. When I ask her what that is, she says it's

'TAKING MONEY OFF IDIOTS WHO HAVE NO IMAGINATION'.

Harmony Hopkinson, my elder sister, is going through a difficult stage – well, that's what I heard Mum saying to her teacher in her *serious* voice.

Harmony treats me like a little sister a bit *too* much. She needs to think more about how she's going to look when these memoirs are published.

She's only happy when she's going off to demonstrate* about something she disapproves of.

Harold Hopkinson is my older brother. He's a bit stroppy and talks a load of codswallop. *And* he gets double-whopper spots on his nose these days. Dad says *he* was like Harold when he was younger, and Mum just says,

'NOW, WHY DOESN'T THAT SURPRISE ME?'

But I really don't know why Dad says he *was* like Harold, because he flipping well still *is*.

We also have a dog called Barkley, who likes eating and going to the park.

He also thinks the poodle who we sometimes bump into is the bee's knees. If he doesn't tone down his BOGGLE-EYES stuff we're going to get into *serious* trouble with the authorities . . .

* DEMONSTRATE –
to shout and scream
like the devil.